A Close Shave . . .

Wright started to tip the barrel of his shotgun up toward Longarm.

Longarm's .45 roared, blowing the barber sheet outward and setting it ablaze where his bullet passed through ahead of its lance of fire.

Carl Wright looked down at his chest, his expression incredulous. Then he glanced over toward the pegs and all the guns hanging against the wall.

"They aren't mine, Carl," Longarm said just as Wright dropped to his knees. And then forward onto his face.

His shotgun clattered hard on the floor, and Longarm flinched, fully expecting the impact to dislodge the hammer and fire the gun. Fortunately there was no discharge. He and the other men in the barbershop began to breathe easier.

DON'T MISS THESE
ALL-ACTION WESTERN SERIES
FROM THE BERKLEY PUBLISHING GROUP

THE GUNSMITH by J. R. Roberts
Clint Adams was a legend among lawmen, outlaws, and ladies.
They called him . . . the Gunsmith.

LONGARM by Tabor Evans
The popular long-running series about Deputy U.S. Marshal
Custis Long—his life, his loves, his fight for justice.

SLOCUM by Jake Logan
Today's longest-running action Western. John Slocum rides a
deadly trail of hot blood and cold steel.

BUSHWHACKERS by B. J. Lanagan
An action-packed series by the creators of Longarm! The rous-
ing adventures of the most brutal gang of cutthroats ever
assembled—Quantrill's Raiders.

DIAMONDBACK by Guy Brewer
Dex Yancey is Diamondback, a Southern gentleman turned
con man when his brother cheats him out of the family fortune.
Ladies love him. Gamblers hate him. But nobody pulls one
over on Dex . . .

WILDGUN by Jack Hanson
The blazing adventures of mountain man Will Barlow—from
the creators of Longarm!

TEXAS TRACKER by Tom Calhoun
J.T. Law: the most relentless—and dangerous—manhunter in
all Texas. Where sheriffs and posses fail, he's the best man to
bring in the most vicious outlaws—for a price.

TABOR EVANS

LONGARM

AND THE SHARPSHOOTER

JOVE BOOKS, NEW YORK

BERKLEY PUBLISHING GROUP
Published by the Penguin Group
Penguin Group (USA) LLC
375 Hudson Street, New York, New York 10014

USA • Canada • UK • Ireland • Australia • New Zealand • India • South Africa • China

penguin.com

A Penguin Random House Company

LONGARM AND THE SHARPSHOOTER

A Jove Book / published by arrangement with the author

For information, address: The Berkley Publishing Group,
a division of Penguin Group (USA) LLC,
375 Hudson Street, New York, New York 10014.

ISBN: 978-0-515-15485-6

PUBLISHING HISTORY
Jove mass-market edition / October 2014

PRINTED IN THE UNITED STATES OF AMERICA

10 9 8 7 6 5 4 3 2 1

Cover illustration by Milo Sinovcic.

Chapter 1

His head had already bounced twice off the ground before he ever heard the gunshot. He remembered coming off the horse but little else. He had had the lead rope of Alton Gray's horse in his right hand, but he could not recall what happened to that horse. Or to his prisoner. Now . . .

Deputy United States Marshal Custis Long lay quiet on the grass. He was comfortable. If anything he was more comfortable now than he could remember ever being. Ever. So comfortable he could not even feel his body.

That seemed off somehow. Not quite right. But he could not work out why. The hit on the head, no doubt.

He looked up at Gray. Longarm lay on his back. Gray stood over him atop the bay horse. The two of them seemed a mile high, sitting there above him.

"Serves you right, you son of a bitch." Gray worked up a wad of spittle and let fly at him.

"Don't try an' get away." Longarm had to pause to catch his breath. "I'll shoot you if you try."

He was short of breath. It was a great effort to speak.

Gray reined the bay horse away and disappeared from Longarm's field of vision. Which at the moment seemed to be directly overhead.

Longarm wanted to sit up. Wanted to scratch his nose, too. He would do those things. In just a minute or so. For the time being he wanted to just lie here on his back and rest.

But the side of his nose did itch quite abominably. He thought he would reach up and scratch it.

But his arm. His hand. He could not feel them. Could not move them. Could not feel . . . anything.

Oh, Lord. He could feel nothing, not anything from his neck downward.

He was paralyzed!

"Hey!"

Longarm's eyelids fluttered and came open despite a buildup of glue-like secretion that bound them closed.

"Son of a bitch. You're alive."

It was a woman. She was standing over him. She had a lead rope in her hand and he could see the head and enormous ears of a mule at the end of that rope.

Longarm was still lying on his back. He had been there . . . he did not know how long. Overnight, he was sure of that. At least one night, possibly more. Time had begun to run together for him as he drifted in and out of consciousness.

"I was . . . never mind," the woman said. She had his wallet in one hand, so she really did not have to explain why she stopped.

"You've shit yourself," she said. "Can't you move?"

He drew in as much breath as he could. "No." The single word came out halfway between a whisper and a croak. "Help . . . me. I'm . . . deputy marshal . . . Long. Help . . . me. Please."

"Well, you damned sure need help. Reckon it's up to me to give it."

The woman was heavy built, stocky, wearing a man's bib overalls and a red pullover shirt. She had a wen the size of a hen's egg on the side of her neck. Her hair, beginning to go gray, was cropped off short just below her ears. He guessed her age to be somewhere in the fifties.

"What am I going to do with you, Deputy Long? I can't leave you here to die." She sighed heavily, as if feeling terribly put-upon. "I suppose I'll just have to take you with me, damnit. Then you'll up and die anyway, but you won't be on my conscience when you do it. So come along, damn you."

She took hold of his coat and half lifted, half dragged him beside the mule. Pushed and pulled and grunted with effort.

Longarm could see a little of what she was doing, could hear grunts and scrapes and the sound of something being dragged across gravel. But he could feel nothing. Absolutely nothing.

He closed his eyes and faded away into unconsciousness again.

Chapter 2

The ceiling consisted of saplings laid close together. He could see thin tendrils of plant roots hanging down between the poles, so the cabin was roofed with sod. The walls were logs chinked with mud.

Longarm could turn his head to the side a little, but that was all the movement he could manage. He could see to the side a bit but could not lift his head to see toward his feet.

The place was small. Eight by eight was his guess. There was a folding, sheet-metal stove; the cot where he lay and a section of pine log about a foot across and two feet high sawed off flat to serve as a stool or a table. That seemed to be the extent of the furnishings.

He wondered how tall the woman was. However tall, she must have been powerful to get him loaded onto the mule and brought here.

She came inside from whatever she had been doing. Pulled off her woolen stocking cap and hung it neatly on a peg driven between two of the wall logs.

"You're awake," she said. "Mayhap you can help me get those filthy clothes off'n you. I got a creek runs by the place. I can wash out your stuff there. In case you're wondering, you been shot. Creased, actually. Right across the back of your neck." While she talked she worked, bending over him, unbuttoning and unbuckling, tugging and lifting and pulling at his clothes.

"Got to wash you, too, lest the stink from you make me vomit. You know how some men down south hunt wild horses? They crease them deliberate. Put the bullet just right, close to the spine it has to be, and it shocks them. Knocks them right down and paralyzes them. Except sometimes they shoot too close to the bone, and it kills them. Sometimes just in the meat not close enough and it doesn't do much of anything to them. But get it just right and they only stay down for a little while. After a spell they stand up, and the horse hunter has them bridled and ready to be broke. Now you, I figure whoever shot you thought he'd killed you. And mayhap he did. You could yet die from this wound. Or you could be up and around tomorrow, next week, one of these fine days. I don't know any way to tell."

While she chattered on, she worked. Pulling his clothes off. Rolling him back and forth so that his cheek was pushed hard against a scratchy blanket first on one side and then the other.

"This water is cold, straight from the creek. Is it too cold for you?"

"No," he grunted. Icy cold or boiling hot, he could feel nothing. He could see that she turned and picked up a basin and cloth and began washing him.

"My God, what a pecker you have, son," the woman crooned. "Bigger even than the candle I've been using to pleasure myself." She laughed, delighted. "What I wouldn't give to have some of that shoved up my twat, eh? Shit, I haven't had a man in . . . let me see . . . three years? Closer to four, I think. Not that you are in much of a condition to be fucking a girl. And more's the pity." She laughed again.

A few minutes later she set the basin aside and said, "That is about as clean as I can get you, but try not to shit yourself any more. It isn't much fun to clean after you."

"Yes, ma'am," Longarm croaked.

"Sleep now. If you're going to heal, that is the best medicine for you," the woman said. "And if you're going to up and die on me after I've brought you this far, do it in your sleep so you won't be bothering me with it, will you?"

She turned away and fed some fat pine into her sheepherder's stove and set a pot of water on top of the stove to heat.

Longarm wondered if she intended to feed him. Or just wait to see if he was going to die before she bothered with that.

He closed his eyes and, taking her advice, went to sleep.

Chapter 3

Her name was Nicole but she went by the name Nic. She had a man's strength and in many ways a man's outlook. She was out here in the mountains, she explained, because this was where the mineral was. Exactly what mineral she was digging she did not say and Longarm knew better than to ask. A direct question like that would have been considered an intrusion on her privacy.

She did feed him. She propped him up in the bed and spooned a little warm broth into him. He did not ask what was in the broth. Suspected it was something he did not want to know. All he cared about was that the broth was warm in his belly and wondrously filling, and he was truly grateful for it.

"More?" he asked when she set the bowl aside. His breath came hard and it was difficult for him to speak.

"No more. You'll shit yourself again," Nic replied.

She did take some warm water from a kettle on the

stove—or boiling for all he could feel—and again dipped a cloth in to wipe his face and chest and cock.

"What are you? Something over six feet, I'd say," Nic mused while she washed him. "Damn good-looking man. It'd be a shame to see you die." She laughed. "Especially with a pecker like that. Why, just look at this thing."

He was lying flat again, she having removed whatever it was she used to prop him up so he could eat. Consequently he could not see exactly what Nic was doing. But he could certainly hear her exclamation of joy.

"Why, will you look at that," she yelped. "You can't feel shit, but your body knows. Damn thing stands tall as a tent pole, doesn't it? Just a minute. Let me see what it tastes like."

Nic bent her head. He craned his neck so he could see a little. She had his cock erect and eager, not that he was aware of feeling anything. She had his foreskin peeled back and was running her tongue around the head.

After only a few moments of that she started bobbing up and down on it. Sucking it, he supposed.

Ugly as Nic was, Longarm nevertheless wished that he could feel her sucking him.

But then at the moment he wished he could feel most anything.

Nic sat up, smiling, and unfastened the straps on the bib of her overalls. When she did that the heavy denim dropped to the floor. Nic stepped out of the trousers. She was naked underneath.

The woman was not fat but she was thick. She had a roll of belly and a dark, curly bush. Her pussy hairs dripped with unspent juices.

Longarm quickly learned why. Still smiling, she joined

him on the bunk, straddling him and lowering herself onto his cock.

He dropped his head back and closed his eyes. Nic, and what she was doing down there, was not a pretty sight.

He could close out the view but not the sounds Nic made as she grunted and wheezed and bounced up and down on his prick until with a cry she achieved her climax.

Finally she climbed off of him.

At least then she had the decency—if he could call it that—to again pick up the bowl of hot water and cloth and once again wash his cock and balls of the juices she had left on him.

"You didn't feel any of that?" she asked.

"No."

"Damn shame, Marshal. I enjoyed it right fine. Filled me up, and there's not many men can do that. We'll do it again tonight, but right now I got work to do." She dressed and over her shoulder called, "Don't you go anywhere, honey."

Nic's laughter was the last thing he heard before the cabin door shut and he was alone again.

Longarm closed his eyes and hoped for sleep. Or for death. Anything other than this uselessness.

Chapter 4

It startled him so much that it woke him up. An itch. A simple little thing like an itch. He could not even be sure *where* he itched. Somewhere down south, that was as close as he could differentiate. In his foot, perhaps, or his leg. But he was sure that it was an itch.

And he could feel it!

"Did you say something, honey?" Nic asked from the stool where she was having her breakfast.

"No." He shook his head. "I di'n say anything."

"Tonight, honey," she said around a mouthful of beans and pork fat. "Tonight we'll have us a fine time." She looked at him. At his crotch, actually. He could see where her eyes were directed. He was still naked. She kept him that way. Liked keeping him naked so she could look at his cock and play with it. And when she had the time could fuck herself with it.

Five days now. He was her own personal dildo, and she had no intention to let her toy get away from her.

He had given up asking for her to go get help for him. Or

to pack him on the back of the mule and haul him out to someplace where there was a telegraph so he could inform U.S. Marshal Billy Vail that Al Gray had gotten away. Again.

Back in Denver, Billy would still be thinking that Longarm was somewhere on the trail. Bringing Gray in for trial. Overdue but somewhere out there.

And Gray. What had become of him while Longarm was laid up here as Nicole whatever-her-name-was's playtoy?

But he definitely had felt an itch somewhere low on his body.

He had never before felt so gloriously wonderful about as simple a thing as an itch, but this one made him feel like rejoicing.

If he had breath enough, he would break out in song. Something good and bawdy. Something loud and happy.

Custis Long chuckled.

And hoped to feel another itch.

Nic finished her bowl of slop and wiped her mouth on the back of her hand. "I'm going to work now, but don't you worry. I'll be back this evening, and we'll have us a fine old time."

The thought made her laugh. It made Longarm cringe. The woman was insatiable. On the other hand, she had saved his life by bringing him back here and feeding him.

"I'll clean you up when I get home, honey. You've shit yourself again. I can smell it."

He could smell it, too. The heavy stink humiliated him almost as much as his immobility did.

But he had felt an itch, an actual, honest-to-goodness itch, and under the circumstances that seemed quite the grand triumph, for where there was an itch there might well be other feeling.

For the first time in days, Custis Long had hope.

Chapter 5

The itch. That damned, miserable itch was back with a vengeance. It was driving him crazy. It was everywhere. Intense and all consuming.

Then, worse, the itch turned to a tingle. Then a burning sensation over every surface on his body.

Longarm cried out aloud, hoping Nic was not close enough to hear. The tingle was just short of being severe pain, and there was nothing he could do to stop it or even to make is lessen.

But he rejoiced in the pain of it because it meant he was *feeling*.

Feeling, even feeling pain, was far better than feeling nothing.

His body was coming back from the shock to his spine that the assassin's bullet had caused.

While he lay immobile on Nic's bunk he had more than enough time to think. He had to conclude that the rifleman, whoever he was, shot Longarm so as to free Al Gray and that he likely believed Longarm was dead. Damn near had been, actually. A quarter-inch difference in the placement of that bullet and he would indeed be dead now.

It was pure luck that he survived, and a man in his line of work could not count on luck.

Longarm craned his neck to look at his bare feet. His whole body felt like it was on fire, but he twitched one big, hairy toe.

And grinned.

He had actually moved that toe.

He did it again and the grin got wider.

He moved a toe on the other foot, then lay back, exhausted by the simple act of holding his head up that long.

Longarm had to admit that he was not in the best of shape after nearly a week flat on his back and with nothing but a few spoonfuls of broth to sustain him.

But by damn he was on his way back. Feeling was returning to his body. He was able to move his toes. With effort and concentration he was able to move a finger as well. And then his hand.

It occurred to him that Nicole was guilty of false imprisonment. And of a federal officer at that.

If he wished, he could arrest her for that and she probably knew it. She was a rough old bat but not stupid. The woman might not want to lose her toy. Might not want him to recover.

Sweating now, Longarm steeled himself against an impulse to move his limbs lest he give himself away. The itching fires that covered his flesh raged, and he could do nothing to stop them.

But, oh, he was able to feel again.

He gritted his teeth to avoid crying out and waited, waited for full movement to return, waited for Nic to return.

Chapter 6

He waited until she had gone out, then got up, found his clothes, and got dressed for the first time in a week. He felt much better when he had boots and clothing and, even more importantly, his double-action, .45-caliber Colt belted around his waist.

It occurred to him now to wonder what had happened to the horse he was riding when the bullet struck Longarm and Alton Gray was a free man again.

Temporarily free, Longarm growled silently to himself. He had been sent to bring Gray back to Denver for trial. And likely for hanging. Deputy U.S. Marshal Custis Long fully intended to do exactly that, never mind that Gray was no longer in his custody.

Longarm had been sent to do a job, and he was going to do it or some son of a bitch was going to die.

Better, he thought, that that son of a bitch be Al Gray or the unseen rifleman than that it be Longarm himself, but the thought of coming up against the rifleman again was not going to deter him. If anything it made him all the more eager. Whoever the bastard was, Longarm wanted a crack at him.

Longarm would take them both in to face the law, Gray and the rifleman, if he could. But if he could not take them in then he intended to take them down. Their choice how that worked out.

He stood, more than a little weak after a week in bed, and swayed from side to side.

Before he could go looking for Gray, he needed something to eat.

He opened the stove door and built up the fire in Nicole's tiny cabin, then rummaged through her things looking for something to eat.

Chapter 7

"What are you doing out of bed?" Nicole gasped when she returned home that evening. "You . . . why didn't you tell me? How long have you been, uh, how long have you been able to get up like this?"

Longarm ignored the questions and said, "I took some o' your food. Don't feel bad about doin' it since you've robbed me of all my money. Now I want it back, all except for a dollar, which oughta cover the cost of the few bites o' grub I've et this afternoon. And mind you, I know how much I had there so don't try an' short me." In fact he had no idea how much had been in his pockets the day he transported Al Gray. But Nic did not know that.

The burly woman—Longarm had known stevedores who would have envied Nicole's biceps—reluctantly dug a purse out of a pile of rags and opened it. She seemed surprised. "It's all there. You didn't take anything."

"I'm no thief," Longarm said. "I coulda found your poke but I had no interest in it. Now give me back what's mine."

"I deserve something for my trouble," Nic whined.

"Yes, an' you already got it. You took it when I couldn't resist nor do for myself. That's true enough. We both of us came out ahead on the deal," Longarm said. "Me with healing, you with, well, you with what you took from me."

The woman, he thought, had about the ugliest pussy he ever saw. And about the strongest appetite to use it. He remembered her expression as she pumped her ass up and down on his cock. That had been pretty ugly, too. All in all, his experience here was not one he would remember with any sort of fondness.

"What happened to my horse?" he asked. "And my hat?"

"I don't know. I never saw no horse. When I found you, you was laying there sprawled out on the grass. There was no horse. Some tracks, but no horse. No hat neither, at least none that I noticed."

Longarm grunted. He was not surprised. Likely Al Gray took the animal with him when he rode away. If not that, then the untended horse simply strayed, maybe heading back to its home or maybe simply wandering from grass clump to grass clump until it was impossibly far away.

It was on loan from the Army Remount Service, and Lord knew where it originally came from.

Losing the horse was only a minor annoyance. But, damnit, he had liked that saddle. He regretted that loss and that of his nearly new flat-crowned brown Stetson.

"You owe me," Nic said. "I gave up my bed and slept on the floor so's you could heal proper."

"You used me for a toy," Longarm accused. "I owe you nothing."

"Where are you going?" Nic asked. "Don't you know it's evening already? Won't you stay one more night?"

"I'm not afraid of the dark," Longarm snapped back at her.

"At least stay and eat with me. We could . . . one more time?"

Longarm ducked his head to get through the door on his way out.

Chapter 8

Longarm's feet hurt like a son of a bitch. He was not sure of the distance from Nicole's mine to Crowell City—some called it Cruel City because of the heartbreak of failed mines in the surrounding hills—but he guessed it to be at least twenty miles and possibly more.

The thing he knew for certain was that it was too damn far. By the time he limped into town he had worn a hole completely through the sole of his right boot and the left one felt paper thin. He could feel every pebble through the worn leather.

It was nearly dawn when he reached the town. Chickens and dogs were awake but not much else.

Longarm spotted the yellow glow of lamplight coming from a storefront in the next block and headed for it.

It was funny, he noticed—funny peculiar, not funny ha-ha—but he had been comfortable enough while he was on the trail hiking in. Now that he had arrived he felt like his feet were close to falling off. And he was so tired he just wanted to lie down somewhere, anywhere, and get some rest.

Funny, too, he mused, but he had been doing nothing *but* resting for the past week. Now he wanted more of it.

He limped on to the lamplight and found it was coming from a café window. The door was latched, but a little tapping on the glass brought the proprietor to open it a crack.

"We're closed, mister. Come back in an hour."

"Look, I don't want t' cause you no trouble, but I been walking all night. My feet hurt an' I'm hungry an' I'm thirsty and those stools by your counter are lookin' awful good to me about now," Longarm said past the crack in the door.

The fellow smiled and shrugged and pulled the door open. "Come in then. The coffee's about ready. I'll get you a cup."

The place seemed to be run by a couple, the man shaggy and his woman worn down before her time. Longarm guessed they were both in their thirties, but the woman looked a good ten years older than her man. She wore an apron and a white cap with flyaway strands of hair poking in all directions from beneath it.

The man immediately poured a cup of steaming coffee and set it in front of Longarm. Only then did he mention, "I got to ask you, mister. Can you pay for your meal? I mean, coffee is one thing. A hot meal is another. If you know what I mean."

"No offense," Longarm said. "I can pay." He pulled a dollar out of his pocket and placed it on the counter.

The café man grunted, turned to his wife, and said something that Longarm could not hear. To Longarm then he said, "Breakfast will be up in a couple minutes."

The pair were as good as their word—well, the man's word, anyway—and quickly laid a spread in front of the dusty traveler. Hotcakes, ham, sorghum syrup, and a dollop of sticky oatmeal, too.

Longarm felt a hell of a lot better once he had that meal in his belly. It gave his gut the feel of a nice, warm glow.

"Thanks, friend." He smiled. "Any idea where I can find a cobbler in this fine community?"

"Glenn isn't a cobbler exactly. More like a saddle maker. But he fixes boots when need be," the café man said.

"An' where would I find this gentleman?"

The café owner gave directions while he made change out of Longarm's dollar. "'Tisn't far," he concluded.

"And a good thing that it isn't," Longarm agreed, thinking of his aching feet.

Chapter 9

Longarm sat at the café counter sipping coffee until well past daybreak until the proprietor mentioned that the saddle maker should have opened his shop for the day.

"Tell Glenn that I sent you," he said.

"Glad to," Longarm told him. "An' you would be . . . ?"

"Buck Walters. Me and my missus run this place." Walters stuck his hand out to shake, and Longarm gave his name. But not his line of work. "My pleasure, Mr. Walters"— a statement of plain fact. His feet still hurt but not nearly as much as when he came in.

Longarm bobbed his head toward Mrs. Walters and touched his forehead in silent salute, then headed down the street and around a corner to find Glenn Farley's saddle shop.

The shop smelled of leather and neatsfoot oil. Farley, a slender man still young but with a body that was twisted and bent, was leaning over a workbench when Longarm came in.

"What can I do for you today?" he asked.

"Buck Walters said you might be able to do me some good." Longarm grinned. "I seem to've worn holes in the soles o' my boots. I like the boots, but I could do without the ventilation in 'em."

Farley nodded. "I can fix that. Do you want new soles or do you want I should do it cheap and just lay a little leather over top?"

"New would be better, I think."

"Yes, but it would cost a dollar a boot. You could get by for half that if you want," Farley said.

"Let's do it right then." Longarm sat on a small bench at the front of the shop and pulled his boots off. The cool air felt good on his feet. He wiggled his toes a bit and handed the boots across to Farley.

"Easy job," Farley said, looking at the boots. "If you don't want to walk around barefoot, I have some old carpet slippers here you can use while I have your boots on my bench."

"That's mighty kind o' you. I'll take them and gladly."

They made the exchange, Farley keeping the boots and Longarm sliding his feet into the oversized but soft and comfortable slippers.

"How long?" he asked.

"They'll be good as new tomorrow afternoon," Farley said.

Longarm had hoped for the work to be done by afternoon, but he was not complaining. He was happy that he could get the work done at all.

And while he was stuck in Crowell City he could ask around and perhaps get a line on where he might find Alton Gray and the son of a bitch who shot him.

Chapter 10

It felt strange to be walking on the town streets wearing carpet slippers instead of his boots. The slippers were soft enough, but the soles were thin and he could feel every pebble and dirt clod that he stepped on.

He found a small hotel that looked clean and went inside. The clerk looked up from a book he was reading and grunted a welcome. "How long will you be here?" he asked.

"Just tonight, I think," Longarm said.

The clerk eyed him suspiciously. "No luggage?"

Longarm shook his head. "My horse ran off with everything I was carrying."

"Tough luck."

"Tell me about it," Longarm responded. He accepted the key to room number four and went upstairs to take a look at it, then back down to tend to some things while he waited on the boots.

First up was a visit to a barbershop for a shave and a bath.

"Know a man name of Al Gray?" he asked the barber.

"No, sir. No one by that name that I can think of," the barber said.

Longarm described Gray but got no better result. He thoroughly enjoyed the bath and the shave, though, and felt considerably better when he walked out of the barbershop than he had when he walked in.

From the barber's he walked down the street to a fairly large mercantile where he bought a shirt, drawers, and socks. The ones he was wearing were becoming ripe. It seemed a shame that Nicole had not washed his things when she had them off.

More importantly he bought himself a hat. The store did not have the snuff-brown model that he favored so he made do with a dove-gray Stetson with a stockman crease. The new hat felt a little strange on his head, but he knew he would soon enough get used to it.

He carried his purchases back to the hotel and put them on, dropping his dirty clothes on the floor.

"Do you do laundry?" he asked downstairs.

"No, but we got a girl comes in every afternoon to collect whatever we have going out, brings it back clean and folded the next morning. If you want something ironed that takes another day. You got something going out?"

"Yes, sir. Up in my room."

"Mind if she goes in there to get it?"

"Not at all. Just give her the key. It's obvious what needs t' be washed."

"It will be ready for you tomorrow, probably late in the morning," the hotel clerk said.

"I thank you, sir. Now where can a man find a drink in this town?" Longarm asked.

The gent gave him directions and Longarm, feeling much better than he had just a little while earlier, headed in that direction.

Chapter 11

"Rye," Longarm said. "The best you have on the shelf there, if you please."

The barman nodded and collected Longarm's quarter without returning any change. He poured a generous measure, though, and the whiskey was excellent. Smooth and pleasant and warm in the belly. Longarm downed the first drink in a hurry, then relaxed a bit and looked around.

He was one of only three customers in the place. It was dark and smelled of spirits and cigar smoke. There was a billiards table in the back and two tables where a man might lay out a game of cards. A tall, narrow table off to the side suggested there might be someone dealing faro but not at this forenoon hour.

One of the other early drinkers took a look, then a second. And then he laughed.

"Mister, if you aren't the miserablest-looking fucker I seen this whole day long," he said loudly.

Longarm took a small sip of his whiskey and ignored the fellow.

"Mister, I'm talkin' to you."

Another sip. "This is good whiskey," he said to the bartender.

"Pay attention when I talk to you, mister," the loudmouth at the bar insisted.

Longarm finally looked at him. "When you have something t' say that I want t' hear mayhap I'll give you that attention. For right now, I just want t' enjoy my drink in peace."

"I'll tell you something you ought to hear. I think you're a pussy, that's what I think. One of those girly boys that likes to suck cock and have it up your ass, coming in here wearing slippers and smelling like a French whore."

That, Longarm realized, was about the concoction the barber smeared on him after his shave. It did smell a little high. Not bad. But there was a lot of smell to it.

Longarm took a deep breath and let it out slowly. He could continue to ignore the son of a bitch. Or he could kill him.

He knew which of those he would prefer. But someone might actually miss him.

Instead Longarm smiled and nodded for the bartender to give the fellow another.

Then he walked over to the belligerent man and cold-cocked him with a sudden right cross.

Longarm looked down at the unconscious man lying at his feet, looked at the fellow's drinking partner, and said, "I've had a hard night, mister, an' I'm not feeling myself at the moment. Tell him that when he wakes up, will you?"

Then Longarm turned and walked out in search of a saloon where a man could drink in peace.

Chapter 12

He had lunch at Buck Walters's café. It was just as satisfying as the breakfast had been. Then he idled along the street, peering into windows and poking among aisles of goods.

As the day progressed the presence of townspeople increased until Crowell City was actually busy. Not busy the way Denver can be but busy enough for a small mining town tucked away amid the peaks and the canyons of the backcountry.

Longarm avoided the saloon where he had that bit of trouble earlier in the day. By five o'clock in the afternoon he was about on his last legs. He was tired after walking all night and getting more and more cranky as time wore on.

Finally he had had enough. He turned and headed back toward his hotel, figuring to turn in for an early night and not even bother with supper.

"You, you son of a bitch," he heard from behind his back.

"You sucker punched me, damn you," the man with the

loud mouth accused. "You couldn't o' done any such of a thing if I'd been expecting it."

Longarm had really had quite enough of the man. He stopped, spun around, and headed back toward the fellow, who was now flanked by two rather large friends. All three of them looked like they had spent the day pouring shots down their throats.

"All right," Longarm snarled. "Now what? You want to tangle? You'd best think twice about it 'cause I am *not* in a very good mood for your kind of bullshit right now."

"You won't do anything this time, asshole," the fellow said. "This time I'm looking straight at you. I know your kind. You are yellow through and through, cocksucker."

Longarm hauled off and coldcocked him once again with a sudden right hand that came out of nowhere and wound up about three inches the other side of the belligerent's jaw.

For the second time that day the man went down, out cold and crumpling to the ground.

Longarm looked at his two companions. "Are you here t' carry the body home? Or do you want t' try me?"

"Mister, we got n . . . n . . . nothing against you. Timothy thought . . . he said . . . well, never mind what he said. Reckon we'll pick him up and cart him off now."

The place they carted Timothy off to, Longarm noticed, was the same saloon they had been drinking in all day long.

With a snort of disgust, Longarm resumed his walk back to the hotel where he had a soft bed just waiting for him to occupy it.

Chapter 13

Longarm woke up groggy, his eyelids glued shut and his head aching. There was daylight streaming through the hotel room window. He sat up on the side of the bed and pondered would it be worthwhile to go downstairs for supper.

Then he noticed the direction the sunlight came from and took out his Ingersoll. The reliable, railroad-grade pocket watch—it was a wonder Nic hadn't stolen that from him; but then she probably had not had a chance to get around to it when he came to—informed him that it was 10:27. And with sunshine showing outside the window, that pretty much had to be the time of morning. He had slept the clock around and then some.

After all that sleep he would have expected to feel fully rested and eager to go. As it was, he felt pretty much like shit.

He stood up and groaned a little. His feet were hurting more than ever, and all he had to put on them were the new socks and borrowed carpet slippers.

"Lordy!" he mumbled as he stood, knee joints cracking, and stumbled over to the washstand.

A splash of water on his face and chest helped. So did a long drink out of the pitcher. He still felt like someone had slipped in during the night and stuffed his mouth with cotton. But there was less of it now. He took another drink, swished it around in his mouth, and spit it into the enamelware basin.

Finally he checked his pockets—a habit—and looked to see that all was right with his .45 before he stepped out into the hallway.

"Good morning, Mr. Long," the desk clerk called when he reached the bottom of the stairs.

"Good morning."

"There is a gentleman who has been waiting for you," the clerk added, inclining his head toward the velveteen furniture at the side of the lobby. "He has been there for quite some time now. Very patient, he is."

"Thanks." Longarm yawned and ambled in the direction the clerk indicated.

"Oh, shit!" he barked when he saw who the visitor was. And what he held in his hands.

It was that son of a bitch Timothy from the day before. And he was holding a shotgun.

He and Timothy locked eyes at just about the same moment.

Timothy reached for the hammer of his double-barrel, fumbled his thumb over it, cursed, and got the hammer cocked and his finger on the trigger.

Timothy's bad luck was that, as fast as he was to cock the shotgun, Longarm's Colt was faster.

Longarm's .45 erupted with smoke and fire, its roar

seeming louder than ever inside the close confinement of the hotel lobby, and a 230-grain solid lead bullet slammed into his upper chest, just about over the point where his heart should lie.

The man was probably as good as dead right there, but Longarm did not take a chance. He fired again, this time his bullet striking Timothy square in the face.

"Jesus," the hotel clerk shouted, clapping his hands over his ears.

"If you can get him here, it probably would be a good thing," Longarm said as he shucked his empty cartridge cases and dropped fresh ones into the cylinder.

"What? What's that you said?" the clerk asked, working his jaw in an effort to unclog his ears.

"Never mind," Longarm said. "Reckon it's too late anyhow. Now," he said, smiling, "where's the best place t' get a meal in this town?"

Chapter 14

Longarm was busy surrounding a plate of steak smothered in gravy when a pudgy fellow wearing a derby and a nickel-plated revolver slid onto the stool next to his.

"I'm not interrupting your meal, am I?" the gentleman asked.

"Not yet," Longarm said around a mouthful of leathery beef. "D'you intend to?"

"Sorry, but I may have to." He stuck a hand out to shake, so Longarm laid down his fork and shook with the man.

"My name is Wilson Hughes. I'm town marshal for Crowell City. Your name is Long?"

"That's right," Longarm said, thinking more about his steak than about Wilson Hughes.

"You're the man who shot and killed Timothy Wright."

"If that was the man's name that I shot this morning, then yes, I'm the one as did that. Did anyone happen t' mention to you that your man Wright laid in wait an' tried t' kill me?

It was purely self-defense. I didn't see that I had a choice," Longarm said.

"Then that will all come out at the inquest," Hughes said, smiling.

"Inquest?"

"Oh, yes. We will have to have an inquest into the death of Mr. Wright," Hughes said.

"I was plannin' on leaving t'morrow morning," Longarm said.

"Yes, after your boots are repaired," Hughes said.

"You seem t' be mighty well informed."

"I try to be." The marshal plucked a pickled pepper off the side of Longarm's plate and popped it into his mouth. "Until the inquest you will have to wait in our town jail." He smacked his lips and took Longarm's last pepper then smiled. "You could, of course, post a surety bond instead."

"An' that bond would be paid to . . . ?"

The man's smile became wider. "Why, to me actually."

"How much are we talkin' about?" Longarm asked.

"A pittance," Hughes said. "Twenty dollars."

Longarm nodded his understanding. And he did, in fact, understand now. Twenty dollars was not a bond, it was a bribe. The money would go straight into Hughes's pocket. "I think we understand each other," he said.

"Then you will want to post bond?" Hughes asked.

"Oh, yes. Let me finish my lunch here an' I'll pay. Where will you be?"

"I have an office over at town hall," Hughes said. "It is just around the corner and one block down. There's a sign outside."

Longarm nodded and picked up his fork again. He used

his knife to saw off another chunk of beef and shoveled it into his mouth. Hughes took the hint and left.

Twenty dollars, Longarm was thinking. Not only was Wilson Hughes a bastard, the man was a cheap bastard.

But his steak and gravy were good, and a bowl of apple cobbler was waiting when he was done with his steak and fried potatoes.

Life could have been worse. Much worse, he thought as he reached the back of his neck and picked at the scab that had formed there.

In fact, he could have had no life left at all.

Chapter 15

Hughes was seated at a rolltop desk when Longarm walked into the town marshal's office. There was not much to the place, the desk and two chairs, a gun rack with a lone shotgun in it, a cast-iron stove, and in the back two prefabricated cells.

"Welcome," Hughes said. "Do you have the, um, bond money for me?" Right to the point, it seemed.

Longarm nodded and dug a gold double eagle out of his pocket. He handed the coin to Hughes, then sat on the chair facing the marshal.

"Oh, there isn't any paperwork involved if that's what you are waiting for," Hughes said. "This is between you and me."

"I got no interest in paperwork," Longarm said. "It don't pay to spread a man's name around." He smiled. "If you know what I mean."

Hughes laughed and reached forward to slap Longarm's knee, a gesture Longarm did not particularly like. "I think I know what you mean, Mr. Long."

Longarm pulled out a pair of cheroots, offered one to

Hughes, who accepted it with pleasure. When both men had their cigars burning, Longarm said, "You might be able to help me find a fellow."

"I might," Hughes said around a mouthful of aromatic smoke. "Who is he?"

"Man name of Al Gray," Longarm said.

"Friend of his, are you?" Hughes asked.

"No, sir, I never met the man. I could stand next to him at a bar an' never know it. This Gray has . . . what you call . . . been recommended to me. As someone who might be able t' help me with a, uh, particular line of work."

"And what sort of work would that be?" Hughes asked.

Longarm gave him a tight smile. "Mine."

Hughes laughed again. "I think I understand you, Mr. Long." He puffed on his cheroot for a moment, then held it a few inches in front of his face as if examining the coal. Finally he said, "I may be able to help you with that. You wouldn't, um, want to help ease my efforts on your behalf, would you?"

Longarm reached into his pocket and produced another twenty-dollar double eagle. He handed the coin to Hughes, who quickly made it disappear into his own pocket.

"Your boots will be ready this afternoon," Hughes said. "Too late for travel then anyway so why don't you come by the office tomorrow, oh, say around ten o'clock. I'll see if I can find some information for you by then. Say, this really is a nice smoke. Thank you."

Longarm stood, touched the brim of his Stetson toward the thoroughly detestable town marshal, and got out of the man's office before Longarm might give in to his true impulses and punch the man square in the face.

Chapter 16

Glenn Farley had the boots ready and good as new when Longarm showed up in the middle of the afternoon. Not only had he replaced the soles, he added new heels and polished them as well.

"You, sir, are a craftsman," Longarm said, meaning it.

"A man is as good as his work, I always say," Farley responded.

Longarm returned the borrowed carpet slippers and very gratefully pulled his boots on again. "Now that feels good," he said with a smile. He stamped his feet a few times to get the tall, black, cavalry style boots settled and smiled again. "Better than new," he said.

It seemed a shame that a man had ended up dying because of the carpet slippers. But then the true cause was not what had been on Longarm's feet—the simple fact that Timothy Wright was an asshole had had something to do with it, too.

Longarm paid Farley for his excellent work and dropped

in at one of Crowell City's saloons for a drink to celebrate the boots. And to waste a little time.

He was interested, if not altogether surprised, by the idea that Wilson Hughes might be able to give him a line on the whereabouts of Al Gray. The corrupt little town marshal would have his sources of information. Longarm's hope was that one of those bits of information might turn out to be where he could find Gray.

Billy Vail had sent him to bring Gray in for trial, and Longarm damn sure intended to do exactly that.

He was, however, running a little short of cash and might be expected to grease the marshal's palm further to get that information about Gray.

"Is there a telegraph in town?" he asked the bartender.

"Ayuh." The man nodded and pointed. "Sensabaugh's got a line. Right next to the post office. You can't miss it."

Longarm grunted. He was always suspicious of any directions that claimed you couldn't miss something because more often than not it seemed entirely possible, even entirely likely, that the desired object could indeed be missed.

Still, the barman's directions were good this time. He found Sensabaugh's Dry Goods and the telegraph desk inside it.

Longarm took only seconds to write out his message but much longer than that to decide what to do with it.

He needed money, and the office would be able to wire funds to him.

But he did not want anyone in Crowell City to know that he was a deputy United States marshal. Sending a request for funds to Billy Vail at the Federal Building in Denver would not exactly seem prudent under the circumstances.

He settled for sending the money request to Henry at his

home address. That should tip them to the fact that he did not want the money to appear to come from official sources without him having to come right out and say so.

NEED FOUR HUNDRED DOLLARS STOP SEND SOONEST STOP THIS ADDRESS STOP SIGNED CUSTIS

No title mentioned nor last name. Now he hoped for two things. One, that they understood. And two, that they authorized the expenditure.

He would know the answers to both soon enough.

"I'll check back with you for my answer tomorrow," he told the dry-goods clerk who took the message form.

"We'll be here," the clerk said cheerfully, reminding him that not everyone in Crowell City was on the far side of the law. A clear majority of the people he encountered here were pleasant, decent, hardworking folk. There were times when a lawman had difficulty keeping that in mind, considering that his daily dealings were mostly with criminals.

"Thank you very much," Longarm said with a tip of his Stetson toward the young man.

He turned and headed back toward the saloon.

Chapter 17

Longarm felt good when he returned to the hotel that evening. He had a hot meal and several shots of rye whiskey in his belly and was well rested after a good night's sleep the previous evening. A fellow couldn't ask for much more than all that.

Except, he realized, one thing.

Like the beautiful young woman walking ahead of him in the upstairs hallway when he came off of the stairs.

Longarm smiled and tipped his Stetson to the lady.

She was tall and slender, probably in her middle twenties or thereabouts with hair the dark gold color of honey. Or good whiskey. She had a long, thin neck, small nose and chin and exceptionally large, blue eyes. Her dress was modestly cut but fitted close to her form, showing that she had small, perky tits and practically no waist at all.

All in all a most handsome lass, he thought as, still smiling, he passed by her in the hallway.

Longarm was almost to his room door when behind him he heard, "Sir. Sir?"

He stopped, turned.

"I'm sorry to bother you, sir," the young lady said, approaching him with a diffident smile.

"No bother, miss," he said, this time removing his hat and holding it in front of his belly. "Is there something I can do for you?"

"There is, actually, if you wouldn't mind."

"Now that," he said, "depends on what 'tis that you'd be wantin'."

The lady blushed. "This is embarrassing, but . . . in my room, sir. I have a portmanteau. I need the contents, and I can't seem to get it open. Could you possibly help me with such a silly thing as that?"

"Of course, miss. Let me take a look at it."

Longarm followed her into her room, which was across the hall and two doors down from his. Her room smelled of some floral perfume and . . . female, some elusively feminine scent that was most pleasant.

He was reminded that it had been some days since he had anything like that to think about. Certainly his experiences with Nic were nothing to remember with fondness.

Now he felt . . . not aroused, exactly. But certainly very much aware of the woman scent and the woman's presence. He thought about turning around and getting the hell out of there lest he embarrass himself with a hard-on. But he had said he would help, and help he would.

"It is right over here, sir," she said, leading him across the room to a luggage stand beneath her window.

The bag was large and black. It was locked shut.

"Do you have the key?"

"No, sir. I have no key."

"Then d'you have a hairpin?" he asked.

The girl smiled. "Now that I do have." She reached up with both hands and did something at the back of her head that caused her hair to cascade over her shoulders in soft waves. When she brought her hands down she was holding several hairpins, which she offered to him.

"I'm gonna ruin one of these," he said. "Is that all right?"

"Yes, of course." Her voice was soft. Very attractive, he thought.

Longarm took one of the hairpins, bent it out more or less straight, and dug into the lock of her bag. A few moments later the lock parted, and the bag was open.

"There y' go," he said. "All fixed."

"Thank you, sir." She stepped close to him and laid a hand on his arm. "If you don't mind me saying it, you are an uncommonly attractive gentleman. Very handsome. Very . . ."

She did not finish the thought. She blushed again. "Would you . . . do you mind . . ."

She moved forward. Came quite naturally into his arms. Lifted her face for his kiss.

Ever the gentleman, Longarm responded in kind. He no longer was concerned about the hard-on that prodded the lady in the belly.

Chapter 18

Melody Thompson was sleek. Body, hair, the way she felt in his arms, she was sleek to look at and sleek to feel. Her body was long and lean. Not at all soft. Her tits were small, her nipples like a pair of tiny, light-pink rosebuds riding on top of them.

For some reason—he did not ask—she cropped her pussy hair so short it almost looked shaved. That allowed her pussy lips to show inside a scant nest of dark hair.

"Beautiful," she exclaimed when she saw Longarm's cock. By then Melody was naked and eager.

She pressed herself against him, one hand cupping his balls as if weighing them, the other stroking his dick. She carefully peeled his foreskin back and ran a long, delicate fingernail around the head.

"So pretty," she said. "So big. I want to feel this inside me."

Longarm picked her up, carried her to the hotel room bed, and gently placed her down. He nuzzled the side of her neck, sucked on her right nipple, moved to cover her.

"You don't have to be so gentle," Melody mumbled into his ear. "I won't break. Go ahead. Pound my belly. I'll love it."

She was already wet and as ready as he was, so he slid his cock inside the wet heat of Melody's thin body. She cried out as he filled her.

Longarm began pumping slowly in and out.

"No," she whispered. "Faster. Harder. Punish me. Do it hard, please. Yes. Harder. Harder."

Longarm pounded her belly with his, moist flesh slapping together, as loud as if he was spanking her tight little ass.

Melody's arms were locked around him and she grasped him with her legs as well. She threw her head back, the tendons in her neck standing out beneath her skin.

"Yes-s-s-s-s-s!" she cried.

Longarm could feel her pussy lips contract and flutter against the base of his cock, clenching tight as waves of sensation swept through her slim body.

He was not yet done. Now he allowed himself to come. And come he did, pouring his juices into Melody's pussy.

The release was so powerful that Longarm, too, cried out aloud, and Melody clutched him tight with her arms as well as her pussy.

"Sweet," she said. "That was so sweet. I loved it. Can we do it again?"

Longarm, still inside her, laughed and acknowledged that yes, they could.

Chapter 19

"Tell me about yourself," Melody murmured. She was nestled in the crook of his arm, her pretty head resting on the side of his chest while she idly picked at his chest hairs.

"Oh, there's not much t' tell," he said, stroking the back of her head. "I'm just a man. Travelin'. Looking around. You know."

She lifted her head and kissed his shoulder, lingering there for a moment before she said, "But that is just the thing. I don't know. I want to know everything about you, Custis Long. Everything."

He laughed. "Careful there or you'll start somethin'."

Melody raised up a few inches. "You couldn't. Not again."

"Keep foolin' around like that an' I will."

"Not possible," she said, more seriously this time.

"Want t' bet?" he challenged.

"Yes. I do," Melody answered. "I say you couldn't possibly. Not again so soon after that last, lovely time."

"Then roll over, woman, an' I'll show you who can do what t' whom."

"On my back?" she asked, her eyes sparkling. "Or on my stomach?"

"Hmm. Like it in your ass, do you?"

"I like it any way I can get it. Do you want me in the ass? That is fine with me. Here." She rolled away from him and moved back close beside him but lying on her stomach, her rather small and tidy butt stuck up in the air.

Melody reached down under her stomach and fingered her wet pussy to pick up some moisture and rubbed it onto her asshole to ease his entry. By then Longarm's erection had returned full force. He moved on top of her. Melody reached back to take hold of his dick and guide it in.

"Slowly now. Give me time to adjust, honey. You're awfully big, you know."

"Too big?"

"Oh, no," Melody said. She giggled. "If anything I would say you are just right in that department."

Longarm pressed forward, felt the head of his cock encounter resistance. Then it burst in, the heat of her asshole surrounding him.

Melody winced once, then pushed back against him, impaling herself on Custis Long's rigid pole. "Yes," she breathed. "Yes, please."

And yes, he pleased her. And himself.

Chapter 20

Melody was still sleeping when Longarm woke and slipped out of her bed. He thought about waking her for one more plunge into that delightful flesh but decided to let her sleep instead. She deserved it after all the effort she had put forth during the night.

He stood, stretched, yawned, then pulled on his clothes and slipped quietly out of her room and down the hall to his own.

Once there he washed and changed to a clean shirt, then went downstairs and out. Buck Walters and his wife provided him with a breakfast big enough to fit a raging appetite.

"Thank you, Buck, Miz Walters," Longarm said, touching the brim of his Stetson to the hardworking pair. He paid and left a generous tip as well. Good people, he reminded himself. Like the Walters family and Glenn Farley. He smiled and silently added, and like Melody Thompson. Now she was good indeed. He almost got another hard-on just thinking about Melody's sleek, supple—and oh-so-hot—body.

He wandered down the street, in no hurry, for a shave and a trim at the barber's. "But leave the mustache, please. I'll trim that myself."

Then down the street to Sensabaugh's to see if his funds had come through yet. They had not, so he ambled on.

He walked over to the livery just to get acquainted with the hostler.

Longarm was more than a little surprised to find both his horse and the one Al Gray had been riding standing in a corral there. Both were borrowed animals, not owned, but he was sure of whose they were.

With that prompting him, he went inside for a closer look. His own McClellan saddle was there, as was the saddle he had borrowed along with the horse Gray had been riding the day Longarm was shot.

There was no sign of his saddlebags and bedroll and he did not want to call attention to himself as a deputy marshal, so he did not ask about them. But he damned sure intended to look for them once he had winkled out the whereabouts of that son of a bitch Alton Gray.

Bringing Gray in was still his priority.

The good news was that, the horses being here, it was entirely possible that Gray was somewhere in or near Crowell City.

Of course it was also possible that after this much time, Gray could be in San Francisco. Or Boston.

Still, the presence of the horses gave Longarm hope that he might yet be able to get Gray back into custody and deliver the man to Denver like he was supposed to.

Longarm felt mighty good when he headed back to Buck's place for lunch.

Chapter 21

Wilson Hughes had said Longarm should check back with him about the same time the next day. After lunch should be close enough, Longarm figured, so he dawdled over his meal, then headed for the town marshal's office.

Hughes was not in, but the door was unlocked so Longarm helped himself to a seat, tipped his hat over his eyes, and laced his hands over his belly while he dozed.

Half an hour later the marshal showed up. "Ah, Long. Just the man I'm wanting to see."

"Marshal," Longarm said, rising and extending a hand. He was careful to hide his true opinion of the corrupt lawman. He would much rather slug the man than shake hands with him, but that would not accomplish anything. Unfortunately. He even managed a smile when he greeted the son of a bitch.

"I was just talking about you," Hughes said.

"With Al Gray?" Longarm asked, hoping. That would mean Gray indeed was still in Crowell City.

"Uh, no. Mr. Gray is, um, not available right now. But his closest associate happens to be. This is someone whose advice Mr. Gray trusts, someone whose advice he takes, in fact. And frankly this is someone who plans most of Mr. Gray's, shall we say, professional activities. If you know what I mean.

"I can arrange a meeting between you and this person, but I was hoping, well . . . to tell you the truth, Mr. Long, I would need some grease on the wheel. If you know what I mean."

Longarm knew what he meant, all right. The slimy SOB wanted another bribe.

Longarm dug into his pocket and came up with a single ten-dollar eagle and some silver.

"Look, the truth is that I'm near about tapped out," he said. "I'm waiting for some money t' be sent to me, but it ain't arrived yet. You can have this if you like. As a down payment, so t' speak. But I won't be able t' come up with anything more until that money arrives."

Hughes smiled, exposing yellowed teeth that reminded Longarm of a coyote, a carrion-eating pest. "Four hundred dollars, I believe the amount is."

Longarm was glad now that he had chosen to avoid using Billy Vail's name or the office address when he sent that wire. Hughes had his tentacles everywhere in town. The game would have been up if Longarm had been open about the addressee of that telegram.

"If my friend has that much t' send," Longarm said. "How'd you know about that anyhow?"

"I keep a close eye on the goings-on in my town," the marshal said. "And I know you will need some of that money for yourself, so let's say I get three hundred and you keep the rest."

"Bullshit," Longarm snorted. "Let's say you get one hundred. I need the rest."

"Two hundred then," Hughes said. "Unless you can do whatever it is you are planning without Mr. Gray's help."

Longarm frowned and fidgeted, then made a show of reluctantly giving in. "All right. Two hundred."

Hughes smiled his carrion-eating smile again and rubbed his hands together. "I'm glad we see eye to eye," he said.

"When will Gray be back?" Longarm asked.

"Soon. That is all I can tell you," Hughes said.

"All you can?" Longarm asked. "Or all you will?"

"All I know myself," the marshal said. "When I find out more I will certainly pass that information along. Is there a, um, a time limit on the, uh, project you need Mr. Gray's help with?"

"It'll hold for a while. Not forever."

"As soon as I know," Hughes said. "In the meantime there is that little matter of my, um, fee."

"When my money comes in, I'll give you half. The other half when you arrange the meet between me an' Gray."

Hughes nodded. "That would be satisfactory, Mr. Long."

Longarm stood, anxious to get out of the marshal's office. He felt dirty just being in the man's company. "As soon as my money gets here, you'll be the first t' know."

The town marshal laughed. "In fact I will," he said. "Maybe even before you."

"For what it's worth, I'm heading over there right now, so you'd best hustle if you want t' beat me to the information."

Hughes laughed again. Longarm reminded himself that it was the last laugh that mattered. And he intended to have that one.

He strode out of the town marshal's office and turned toward Sensabaugh's Dry Goods.

Chapter 22

"That's right. Long. Custis Long. An' no, I don't have any identification t' prove that."

"We're supposed to get identification before we pay out this much money, Mr. Long," the clerk insisted.

Longarm gave the dry-goods clerk, who doubled as telegraph agent, a dirty look. "Sonny, you're the one that took my message down t' send, asking for this money."

The truth was that he did indeed have the sort of identification that the young man was asking for, but it proved he was Deputy U.S. Marshal Custis Long. And wouldn't town marshal Hughes be interested in that tidbit of information. Hughes would probably give the telegrapher a bonus for that.

"All right," the clerk finally said. "But you will have to sign a statement testifying to your name."

"Get out your papers then. I'll sign 'em."

Ten minutes later Longarm had his cash in hand. Billy Vail, bless his heart, had sent five hundred dollars instead of the four hundred that had been requested. And he did not even know why Longarm wanted that amount of cash. Now that, Longarm thought, was a splendid boss.

From Sensabaugh's he went back to the town marshal's office and delivered five double eagles to the scumbag.

"Remember," Longarm cautioned him. "You get the other hundred after you put me an' Al Gray together. An' the sooner the better."

"I can't introduce you to Mr. Gray until he gets here, Mr. Long. Surely you understand that. At the moment he is what you would call away on business."

"I understand business, Hughes. I got business o' my own with Gray. Surely you understand that. Now if you'll just give me a receipt for that money I just gave you."

Hughes gave him a stricken look, his eyes bulging and jaw dropping.

Longarm roared with laughter. "Reckon I got you this time, didn't I?"

"I, uh, yes. You did, Mr. Long. Can I buy you a drink? To, um, celebrate our business deal?"

"Thanks, but I got something I need t' do this afternoon," Longarm said. Actually he just did not want to have anything to do more than was strictly necessary with the sleazy marshal. Certainly he did not want to drink with the man. "You'll let me know when Gray gets back, right?"

"Immediately," Hughes promised.

Longarm grunted a good-bye and got out of there. The very idea of having to drink with a man like Wilson Hughes made him angry.

Spending some time with Melody Thompson, now that was a different notion altogether. He would have to see if she was free for a little playtime this afternoon.

Chapter 23

"Sorry, Mr. Long. Miss Thompson checked out this morning. And before you ask, she did not say where she would be going."

Longarm sighed, then thanked the hotel desk clerk.

"I can get you another girl," the clerk said, lowering his voice and glancing over his shoulder. "Just as good as Miss Thompson and not as expensive."

"Not as . . . expensive?" Longarm said, not taking the man's meaning for a few seconds.

The clerk in turn failed to appreciate the reason for Longarm's confusion. "Only five dollars. Ten for all night," he said. "And the girl I have in mind is really quite beautiful. I'm sure you would like her." The man smiled. "Would you like for me to arrange for her to come to your room? You wouldn't have to be seen in public with her, if that is what you are thinking."

"I, uh, no. I mean . . . I'll let you know later if I want her. This girl you have in mind, would she, um, does she work for the same people as Miss Thompson?"

"No, sir. Miss Thompson doesn't work for a house. She

has a, uh, a special friend, as she puts it. A man, of course.
But the two of them come and go. Her gentleman friend is
away at the moment, which I know for a fact. Otherwise he
would have been the one to arrange for you to have her company," the clerk said.

Shee-it! Longarm thought. Melody was a whore. She had
a pimp. But last night . . . what the devil was that all about?
Certainly she never mentioned money. He'd had no idea who
she really was.

Longarm had no illusions about his own looks. Oh, it
was true enough that he had no trouble finding pussy.
Women seemed to think his rugged looks were attractive
enough. But whores? Why in the world would a working
girl approach him, give him a delightful night of fucking
and sucking, yet never so much as mention payment?

That did not seem reasonable. Certainly a whore would
not be in the game just for the fun of it.

At least he did not think that seemed reasonable. Melody
seemed a smart girl, competent and capable. And damned
good in bed. If all she wanted was a roll in the hay, she could
get that professionally.

In his experience, whores did not generally give free
samples.

Was she setting him up for something? For what? And
if she was, why disappear now?

Longarm grunted. Smoothed the ends of his mustache.
Turned around and headed for the street.

He had many more questions than answers. If he kept this
up, he decided, he was just going to give himself a headache.
Better, he thought, to go have a drink, maybe find a friendly
card game. For sure he wanted to quit thinking about Melody
Thompson and the many possible reasons for her actions.

Chapter 24

The saloon seemed more whorehouse than drinking establishment. There were eight or nine of the soiled doves fluttering around the place in their short dresses and feathers, and he had had just about enough of their sort for the time being. He was still not over the surprise of learning about Melody.

On the other hand the bar served a decent brand of rye. And they were cheap. The place was a bit house, meaning any drink you ordered cost only a bit, two drinks for a quarter or thirteen cents if you only wanted one.

Longarm laid down a half dollar. "Rye whiskey," he said. "Beer chaser."

The rye was good on the tongue and warm in the belly, and the beer was crisp and pleasant.

"Cigar?" the bartender offered.

Longarm smiled. He was definitely beginning to like this place with its low ceiling and dark walls. A man could lose himself here, and that was just exactly what he intended.

Half an hour later he was giving thought to supper. Buck Walters was not open for the evening meal. He and his wife started early but closed their café in midafternoon, so that was out.

In the meantime there was the free lunch spread to assuage his hunger. Longarm reached for a pickled egg and started to munch.

"Are you Long?" The question sounded more challenge than simple inquiry.

Longarm turned. Saw a short, stocky man with a receding hairline. Receding jaw, too, or so it appeared. This fellow would have an unfair advantage in a fistfight, Longarm thought; he didn't have a chin to punch.

"I'm Long," Longarm admitted.

"You murdered my brother," the man accused.

"Y'know, neighbor, I don't recall murdering anybody real recent," Longarm said, fashioning a smile and placing the remains of his egg down on the bar.

"Does the name Timothy Wright mean anything to you?"

Longarm nodded. "He's the fella as tried to kill me over in the hotel lobby. Laid in wait for me with a shotgun an' an attitude. I shot quicker an' straighter. Let me ask you something. You got any more brothers?"

Wright looked puzzled. "Why would you ask that?"

"T' see if I got t' watch over my shoulder for any more o' you Wright boys after I've done with you," Longarm said. He straightened, putting his back to the bar. "What will it be? Are you gonna make me shoot you, too?"

Wright hesitated. For a moment Longarm thought he was going to go for the pistol on his hip. Instead he looked like he was about to cry. His face flushed dark red and he began to shake. With a stifled cry he turned and walked, practically fled, out of the saloon and into the street.

With a sigh, Longarm turned back to the bar. He did not want what was left of the egg after it was lying on the bar so he reached for another. Good eggs, he thought. Tasty.

Chapter 25

Bad luck. Longarm was trying to avoid Wilson Hughes, and the son of a bitch walked into the same saloon where Longarm was trying to enjoy a quiet drink or two.

"Ah, there you are, Long," Hughes said, showing his teeth in a wolfish grin. He joined Longarm at the bar, uninvited. "I thought you said you had things to do this evening."

"Yes, and I done 'em," Longarm returned. He had been about to leave the saloon and look for a bite of supper, but he definitely did not want to have the marshal for company. Instead he ordered another drink.

"Make that two," Hughes said. "On my tab, Jesse."

"Yes, sir, Marshal," the bartender said. It seemed that Hughes was a regular at this saloon. But then for all Longarm knew, the bastard might be a regular at every saloon in Crowell City.

"Mr. Long can't buy a drink tonight, Jesse. He's drinking on me."

"Yes, sir."

Longarm gritted his teeth and lifted his fresh rye in Hughes's direction. "T' your good health, Wilse," he said. "Any news about that, uh, matter we was discussin' earlier?"

"No, not yet, but don't you worry. As soon as he gets back, I will know it, and I will set up something between the two of you. You have my word on that, and my word is my bond. Anyone in Crowell City can tell you that."

Right! Longarm thought. *Your word is as good as gold . . . unless someone crosses your palm with some gold. Then you bow to the highest bidder, Wilson. Oh, I do know your kind.*

Longarm downed his rye—it seemed a shame to toss it back like that when it deserved to lie on the tongue for a moment so he could savor the liquor properly—and hitched up his trousers.

"Excuse me, Wilse. There's something I need t' do. But thanks for the drink. They serve good stuff here." Longarm tugged the brim of his Stetson a little tighter, nodded to Hughes, and headed for the door.

He was three steps out onto the boards of the sidewalk when he heard the unmistakably nasty click of a firearm hammer being cocked.

Chapter 26

Without taking time for thought, Longarm immediately dropped facedown. By the time he hit the boards his .45 was in his hand.

He heard a roar and felt the passage of a hot wind across the back of his neck, which still bore a scab from the last time someone tried to dry gulch him.

From off to his left he heard a plaintive, "Oh, Jesus. I've missed the son of a bitch."

He looked up to see Timothy Wright's brother trying frantically to reload a shotgun, perhaps even the same shotgun his brother used in his failed assassination attempt.

Thoroughly disgusted with the Wright clan, Longarm stood, transferred the Colt to his left hand, and with his right began brushing away some of the dried mud that many passing boots had left on the wooden sidewalk.

"You'd best quit tryin' to reload that fowling piece, mister. If you do manage t' get it charged again I'll prob'ly have t' shoot you. I mean, one family only is entitled to so damn many tries at killing me. Pretty soon you're either gonna do it . . . or make me really pissed off. Now drop that smoke pole. Yes, damnit, and the shells for it, too."

Longarm walked over to the man and slapped him across the face. He did not punch him since there was so little, undersloping chin to aim at. He simply slapped the idiot. Like a woman might except Longarm's backhanded slap was enough to rock Wright back on his heels.

With a snarl and a curse, Longarm bent down and retrieved the shotgun. It was a double barrel, far from new with whatever bluing it might once have had long since worn off.

Without a word, Longarm handed the gun back to the startled man.

"But . . . I thought . . ." Wright leaned over to pick up the fallen shotgun shells, but Longarm stopped him, touching his wrist with the side of his boot. "You don't need them things," Longarm said. "Not 'less you see a squirrel here-abouts, an' I don't think you're likely t' do that. Now take your damn gun an' go."

Wright turned but after he had taken a step or two, Longarm said, "Wait a minute. There's something I got t' ask you. Is that the same gun your brother tried to use on me?"

Wright stopped, stared at him for a moment, and then, shoulders slumped, resumed walking away.

By rights Longarm could have arrested the man. Or killed him. Neither seemed worth bothering with.

Longarm continued on in his search for a decent supper.

Chapter 27

Longarm slept alone that night. He would have preferred the company of Melody Thompson, whore or not, but the room she had occupied was empty, the door to it standing ajar—he had checked, hoping to find her there—and her belongings gone.

In the morning he walked down to Buck's café for breakfast, then over to a barbershop where he joined a half dozen men who were in line for shaves.

He picked up a two-month-old New York newspaper and pretended to read it while he eavesdropped on the conversations around him.

The men spoke quietly, mostly about mining, using terms like "yield per ton" and "rock strata."

Longarm knew that most hard rock mining camps had short lives. They boomed wildly and were flush with money but only until the valuable ores that supported them began to fail. Soon thereafter the population declined, and the town began to shrink. Most eventually faded away completely and became ghost towns.

The western mountains were thick with abandoned towns, the men who once had flocked to them long gone, and only shadows and memories remained.

"Just the shave," Longarm said when his turn in the chair came. "I'll take care o' my own mustache."

"You're new in town," the barber observed while his hands flew back and forth, stropping his razor.

"Yes, sir."

"Mining man, are you?" The barber finished sharpening the razor and began whipping soap into a lather.

"Just passing through," Longarm said.

"Lots of mining engineers come through here," the barber said. "Are you . . . ?"

"No."

"You're dressed like you might be an engineer. You aren't a working stiff, I can see that. Likely not a gambler, either. And you're not a stockman bringing beef up from the lowlands. Not wearing low-heeled boots, you aren't. Are you—"

"I'm a man as likes t' mind his own business," Longarm cut the garrulous man off.

"Oh. Sorry." He began smoothing lather onto Longarm's cheeks. The remainder of the brief time Longarm spent in the chair was silent.

When he got out onto the street again, Longarm chuckled softly to himself. The barber had spanked him for not being chatty. The son of a bitch had neglected to splash aftershave onto him when he was done. Instead of being angry, Longarm was amused by the petty little show of pique.

But he would not be using that barber again if he was in Crowell City long enough to need another shave.

He wondered if there was any point in walking over to the town marshal's office to see if there was any word yet about when Al Gray would get back. Probably not. But he had nothing better to do anyway.

He tipped his Stetson back on his head and ambled in that direction.

Chapter 28

"Long. Mr. Long. Wait."

Longarm stopped and turned to see Marshal Hughes scurrying up the street after him. The marshal was puffing and flushed.

"Wait. I have some information for you," Hughes said as he came near.

Longarm glanced around, then leaned against the front wall of Walker's Mercantile. "Yes, Marshal? Have you heard from Gray about when he'll get back?"

Hughes reached Longarm and stopped. He bent over and rested his hands on his knees for a moment while he sucked in deep breaths. "Ah. I'm out of condition," he complained. "There was a time when I could run like a deer." He looked up and laughed. "But that was quite some time ago."

"You was saying something about Al Gray?" Longarm prodded him.

"Yes. Of course. I didn't hear direct from Mr. Gray, but I did hear about him. It seems that, uh, Mr. Gray has been detained. In a county jail, actually. Over in Wynn County. He was arrested on a charge of drunk and disorderly and did not have the wherewithal to bail himself out. So he is not expected back here now for more than a week. I thought it only fair to tell you. Naturally I still intend to complete our bargain. When Mr. Gray does return, I will be glad to put you two gentlemen together."

"Thank you for tellin' me, Wilse. More than a week, you say?"

Hughes nodded. "So I am told, yes."

"All right, thanks. I may mosey along an' take care of some other business while we're waitin' for Gray t' get back here," Longarm said.

"Yes, of course, and you will have the remainder of my, um, fee at that time?"

"I said I would," Longarm said.

"Very good. Thank you." Hughes gave him a carrion eater's grin and rubbed his hands together.

Longarm turned and resumed walking. But not with his original intent. He knew very well Sheriff Bob Kane in Wynn County. Bob would be happy to turn the prisoner over to Longarm for delivery to the courts down in Denver.

Longarm's next logical move, he thought, would be for him to go over to Wildwood, the county seat there, and collect his man after someone else had done the work of finding him. Longarm smiled to himself. Perhaps he should pay Wilson Hughes that other hundred dollars since he had made the arrest so easy.

Not that he seriously intended to do that. He was already thinking about how he should describe the first hundred dollars of bribe money on his expense report.

He walked down to the livery where his strayed horse seemed to have found a new, if somewhat illegal, home. It was not a terribly far ride over to Wildwood. Longarm intended to hire a horse here in Crowell City and make the trip.

Chapter 29

·

The horse the livery gave him was hardmouthed and sassy. It would not hold a gait and constantly wanted to reach down and crop grass while it was moving. It had a vile disposition and spooked at every bush or shrub they came to. In short, it was what Longarm was accustomed to borrow from the Army Remount Service; certainly it was no worse than his usual mounts.

Even so it carried him the thirty or so miles from Crowell City to Wildwood in less than the day. He reached Bob Kane's office in the Wynn County courthouse late in the afternoon.

"Custis Long!" Kane yelped when Longarm walked in. The tall, lanky sheriff jumped up from behind his desk and raced to pump Longarm's hand in an enthusiastic greeting. "Damn but it's good to see you, old son. It's a very pleasant surprise."

"Good t' see you again, Bob," Longarm said with a broad smile. "How long has it been?"

"I know exactly how long it has been," Kane said.

Longarm's eyebrows went up in surprise at that statement.

Kane laughed. "It has been exactly too long."

"Now I can agree with you 'bout that," Longarm said.

"What brings you out our way, Custis?" Kane asked.

"Fella name of Alton Gray. I believe you have him in your jail. I want him."

Kane shook his head. "I don't have anyone by that name, Custis. I've seen the flyers on him, and I would have held him for your people if I had caught him."

"I was told you had a man here on drunk and disorderly, was serving ten days or something like that," Longarm said.

The sheriff shook his head again. "No, no one by that name. I did have a fellow, called himself John Amos, but he bonded out yesterday. What does your Gray look like again?"

Longarm described his recent prisoner.

"Damn," Kane grumbled. "That was Gray that I had, all right."

"You say he bonded out?"

"That's right. Or to be more accurate about it, he was bonded out but not out of his own pocket. A woman came and paid his bond. Paid for the damages he caused over at Pete Vold's saloon, too. Good-looking woman. Makes me wonder how a piece of slime like Amos . . . or Gray, I suppose . . . corralled one like that. But then some women are attracted to ruffians, and it seems like the classier the woman the worse the scoundrel she is with."

"Aye, does seem like that sometimes," Longarm said. He laughed and added, "Bein' something of a no-good myself it's the only way I can get hold of any women. Any idea where Gray an' this woman friend went from here?"

"No, but I know they went in different directions. The woman took a stagecoach. Amos—Gray, I mean—rode off on horseback."

"His own horse?" Longarm asked.

"I suppose so. I didn't ask," Kane said.

"So you don't know where he kept the horse while he was behind bars?"

"We only have two livery stables in Wildwood. It would almost have to have been with one of them. I suppose the woman paid for that, too, or the horse would have been impounded and put up for me to sell," Kane said.

"I'll have t' ask them," Longarm said. "Maybe they have an idea of where he's gone."

"I'll take you over and introduce you," Kane said. Then he grinned. "But afterward I insist that you come home and have your supper with Leanne and me."

"Now that's the best offer I've had all day," Longarm said, smiling. "Come along then, old friend. We have a lot of catching up to do."

Chapter 30

A man named Fischer at Zachary's Livery had a partial answer for them when Longarm and Kane inquired about Gray.

"Mr. Amos? Sure, I remember him. Kept his horse here and ran up quite a bill for the board. I was beginning to worry that I might have to put the animal to auction, but a lady came along and paid. Paid to the last cent and even gave me a tip above what was owed," Fischer said.

"Did either of them say where Amos would be going from here?" Longarm asked.

"No, sir. But then I didn't ask. I don't figure it's any of my business where folks come from or where they go. I only chatter about stuff like that to be friendly. It isn't like I really care. Sometimes people say but most often they don't. I wish I could help you, but I just don't know anything. Is this Amos fellow a famous outlaw or something?" the liveryman asked.

"Not famous, but he's working on it. He's wanted by the

federal government. We're trying to stop him from causing enough hurt that he becomes famous," Longarm said.

"Thanks for your help, Jerry," Kane said.

"Anytime, Sheriff. You know you can count on me to help any time I can," Fischer said.

"And that seems to be that," Kane said as they walked away from the livery stable. Then he smiled and said, "Are you ready for a fine meal? I sent word home, so Leanne will be expecting us. She likely has the table set and supper ready."

"You can't know how much I'm looking forward to it," Longarm said. It was good to be himself again.

"Will you stay the night?" Kane asked.

Longarm shook his head. "I don't think so, Bob. Thanks, but I'll take a room at the hotel. I'll want to spend some time with the cards and have a drink or two, an' I know Leanne is set against having liquor in her house. I wouldn't want t' make her uncomfortable."

Kane nodded his understanding and took no offense at the refusal. He grinned. "I hope she's had time enough to bake one of her famous rhubarb pies."

"Lordy, I hope she has, too," Longarm said. He had had Leanne Kane's specialty pie a time or two before.

Both men extended their strides at that prospect.

Chapter 31

"Turn your head, Bob. You shouldn't be lookin' at this," Longarm said before he leaned down and gave Leanne a light kiss on the cheek. "Thanks, Leanne. The supper was wonderful."

"Anytime, Custis. And next time if you give me a little more notice I'll have that rhubarb pie that you like," the lady said.

"In the meantime you can practice making it," Bob Kane said.

"Oh, you. You would have me baking rhubarb pie every night if you could," she said, laughing.

"Not a bad idea," Kane said.

"You two can work that out later. In the meantime I'll take my leave," Longarm said, "and truly, I do thank you. Supper was the best I can remember in ages." He turned to Kane and extended his hand to shake.

"Will I see you again before you go?" Kane asked.

"I may stop by the office in the morning for a little

coffee before I get on the road back to Crowell City. My man is supposed to go back there. At least I hope he does. I haven't told Billy that I lost the son of . . . oh." He looked over at Leanne, who was hearing this conversation, and stopped short of what he had been about to say.

"Anyway, I haven't told Billy yet," he finished.

"Do you want me to tell him for you?" Kane offered.

"I don't think so. I don't know what circuit these tele-graph lines are on. Might be that Crowell City can read traffic coming out of Wildwood, and I know the operator over there spills everything he hears to the town marshal, an' that man is bent in the wrong direction. He must be makin' a fortune off the bribes he collects."

Leanne had drifted back into her kitchen. Longarm looked to make sure the door was closed, then said, "The son of a bitch seems t' have some sort of accomplice, too. Bastard shot me a week or two ago. Likely thinks I'm dead, an' I'd just as soon he keeps on thinkin' that until I can fig-ure out who he is an' nab him, too. Assault on a fed'ral offi-cer should get him about five to ten in Leavenworth to go along with Al Gray's sentence. Maybe the two o' them can bunk together in prison."

"If your man shows up back here, I'll grab him for you," Kane promised.

"Thanks, Bob." Longarm shook the sheriff's hand again and said, "Dinner was even better than I remembered, and Leanne is even prettier. G'night now."

Longarm turned toward the hotel where he had left the few things he brought with him from Crowell City.

He made a stop first, though, at the One Horn Steer for a drink or three, played a little poker, had another drink or two.

And succumbed to the charms of a little floozy who called herself Rose.

The girl was small, probably not standing more than five feet tall when she was wearing high-heeled shoes. She had coal-black hair that hung short and straight, dark eyes, and a dusky skin tone.

She was also very subtle. She walked over to Longarm and planted her palm on his crotch to feel what he had in there. When she discovered the size of him she shrieked and said, "You have the one horn, honey, but you're no steer. Now the question is, do you have a dollar?"

"One dollar, eh. What would you do for two?" he asked.

"Darlin', pay me two dollars and I'll fuck you clean into the ground. I'll drain you so dry you won't be able to walk. It will take two strong men to carry you down from my room," she returned.

"Prove it," Longarm challenged, laughing.

Rose took his arm and led him up the stairs.

Chapter 32

Rose's crib was almost as tiny as she was, but she had taken some pains to decorate it with wallpaper and artificial flowers. A blanket was laid over the foot of the narrow bed. That was to keep the bed from being soiled by gentleman callers who chose to keep their boots on.

Gentle men? Longarm doubted that. Men, certainly. But gentle? Not likely, as attested by a large bruise beneath Rose's left tit.

The girl stripped her dress off in one well-practiced motion and matter-of-factly began helping him to unbutton and shuck his clothing as well.

Rose was pretty in an elfin, little-girl way. She had a thin, heart-shaped face with a small nose and long eyelashes, very large, dark eyes, and rounded cheeks.

Her belly was flat and her waist so small as to seem almost nonexistent. Her tits were small, firm cones that stood tall and proud, her nipples tiny and dark brown.

She got his clothes off and for a moment looked worried.

"Honey, I don't know if I can take all of that into me. Lordy, I can't remember ever seeing a pecker that big." She giggled. "But I'm looking forward to give it a ride. First, though, do you mind . . . ?"

Rose perched on the edge of the bed and leaned forward. She took Longarm's cock in her hand and moved it from side to side, up and down, admiring it from all sides.

She peeled his foreskin back to expose the red head of his cock and took it into her mouth. She pushed down, trying to take it all into her throat, but she gagged and quickly withdrew, coughing.

Rose looked up at him. "Sometimes I can do that," she said, "but you're just too big." She grinned. "Bet I can take it in my pussy though."

"Let's find out," Longarm said.

He reached down to take Rose in his arms. He lifted her, stretched her out flat, and lowered her gently onto the bed.

Longarm nuzzled her tits and lightly sucked on her nipples, which turned hard and erect.

"Lie down for a minute, honey," Rose said. Longarm complied and she began licking his nipples, then his belly and his balls. Finally she ran her tongue up and down the length of his dick and around and around the head of it.

"About that ride you promised me," he said.

"I always deliver what I promise, honey," she responded, straddling his waist and easing slowly down onto his cock until the warmth of her surrounded him.

Longarm smiled. "Reckon you can take all of it after all," he said.

"It feels good in there, honey," Rose told him. "Awful good." She began moving up and down on him, at the same time rotating her hips. She braced herself on his chest and began moving faster, driving herself down onto him, working hard at it, gasping, eyes closed and head thrown back until the tendons on the side of her neck and the veins there stood out beneath the skin.

Rose squealed and shuddered, reaching a climax moments before Longarm shot his sperm into her pussy.

She collapsed onto his chest, stretching out and lying on top of him. Her breath was rapid and uneven. After a moment she said, "I didn't expect that, honey. It was nice. Thank you."

"The pleasure was all mine," Longarm told her.

Rose chuckled. "Not all of it, believe me." She sighed and said, "I've been with a lot of gentlemen, but you're special."

Longarm stroked her back and her hair. He knew better than to believe such compliments from a working girl. But it was nice to hear anyway.

He left his cock inside her and after a few minutes it began to swell with renewed interest. Rose felt the change, too. She kissed his throat and began slowly to move her hips.

She was smiling.

Chapter 33

"You look like you didn't sleep well last night," Bob Kane told him over coffee early the next morning. "Was there something wrong with the room?"

"The only thing wrong with it was that I didn't get into it sooner," Longarm said. "Not that I'm complaining, mind you. I had a pretty good reason for not getting there."

"I won't ask what that reason was. Or, rather, who it was," Kane said, laughing.

Longarm took a swallow of the hot, bitter coffee and said nothing. But his smile said volumes.

Bob had brought some of Leanne's homemade crullers for Longarm to take with him on the ride back to Crowell City, but the men ate them with their coffee instead.

"Reckon I'd best be moving along," Longarm said.

"I notice you don't think of that until all the crullers are gone," Kane said.

"Hell, Bob, I'm not stupid."

"I can't tempt you with another cup of coffee?"

"No. Thank you, but no. I don't want t' be too late getting in there," Longarm said. He stood and stretched, yawning, then extended his hand to Kane. "Give my love to your bride."

Kane remained behind in his office while Longarm walked over to the livery stable to get his rented horse. When the hostler brought the animal out to him and Longarm reached into his pocket to pay, the hostler said, "No charge, sir. Sheriff Kane said the board bill is to be charged to the county."

"Thank him for me, would you, please?" He gave the man a half-dollar tip and swung into the saddle to start the ride back to Crowell City and, hopefully, to a meeting with fugitive Al Gray.

He nooned beside a tiny rill of sweet water and made a lunch off a handful of venison jerky he had brought along, thinking back to the excellent meals Bob Kane's wife could cook, that rhubarb pie in particular. It seemed a damn shame that she had not known he was in the vicinity in time for her to bake one this trip.

Next time, he promised himself.

But this time . . . Al Gray.

Chapter 34

Getting back to Crowell City was not exactly like homecoming. The truth was that he did not much care for the town. Longarm admitted to himself that his view of the town was shaded by his view of Wilson Hughes, and while that might not be fair it was just the way things were.

He returned the horse to its owners at the livery and paid for its use out of his pocket. Usually, of course, that was an item that he would simply issue a voucher for payment. But the vouchers against the federal government were not exactly something a traveling crook would have, and as far as anyone here knew that was what he was. Deputy U.S. Marshal Custis Long did not exist here. Yet.

He carried his meager belongings back to the hotel and upstairs. There still was no sign of Melody Thompson. He checked and was disappointed to find her room empty. His room seemed undisturbed since he left it.

Longarm washed and went back downstairs in search of supper, which he found at the first place he came to. He ate quickly if not particularly well and headed for Bresler's Saloon, where they had fresh beer and reasonably smooth rye.

He was halfway there when a lance of yellow flame and white smoke pierced the twilight ahead of a loud roar.

Longarm heard more than felt the patter of something striking his tweed coat and stinging his belly.

His .45 appeared in his hand without conscious thought as he reacted to the assault.

The shot had come from an alley a hundred feet to his front. He snapped a shot in that direction, knowing there was almost no likelihood that it would connect with whomever it was that shot at him. He saw a spray of wood chips fly off the corner of Hatton's Sundries.

With the Colt in his fist, Longarm dropped into a crouch and charged straight at the alley.

A second blast followed the first, this one going somewhere astray. He did not know who or what might have been hit by that shot, but it did not come close to him.

Again he followed the attacker's fire with a shot of his own. He fired while he was still running and was fairly sure his bullet came nowhere near the man who shot at him.

Longarm heard footsteps receding through the alley. By the time he reached it and could see down its length, the gunman was gone, out of sight to either left or right at the far end of the alley.

He stopped, leaned against the side wall of Hatton's, and took time to reload the two chambers he'd already fired.

Only then did he start his stalk through the alley.

Chapter 35

Longarm reached up with his left hand, touched the new skin on the back of his neck where the unknown rifleman had creased him. The scabs were all gone now and he assumed the skin there would still be red and raw. One thing he knew for sure was that this being shot at was a bunch of bullshit. He'd had quite enough of it.

He reached the end of the passage between Hatton's and the haberdashery on the other side. The son of a bitch with the shotgun could have gone in either direction.

His assailant almost had to be Timothy Wright's brother. Longarm could think of no one else in Crowell City who might want him dead. Al Gray would, but Wilson Hughes would warn Longarm before Gray returned. Certainly no one other than Wright would be fool enough to come at him with a shotgun. And to shoot from so far away that the shot pellets had so little effect.

The man was not terribly bright. Nor had his now dead brother been.

But where was the surviving Wright now? That was the question.

Longarm normally carried only five cartridges in his Colt and the hammer down on an empty chamber. That way there was no chance of an accidental discharge.

In the past he had seen more than one unlucky son of a bitch who accidentally shot himself by dropping his gun. And one especially unfortunate bastard whose horse kicked him, the animal's hoof striking the hammer of his Colt and firing a bullet into the poor sap's leg.

Now he flicked open the loading gate and dropped a sixth .45 cartridge in. Just in case.

He did not really think Wright would have the nerve to stand up to Longarm face-to-face. But he could be wrong about that. This situation could come to a gunfight, and if it did, he would want that sixth cartridge in the cylinder rather than in his coat pocket.

He took his hat off and peeked warily around the back corner of Hatton's. There was no sign of Wright in the growing shadows in that direction, so Longarm looked the other way. Nothing there, either.

It was nearly dark, and Longarm was not familiar with the town's back alleys. At close quarters a shotgun is a devastating weapon. Both good reasons to back off and wait.

Custis Long was not very good when it came to backing off.

It looked like he was going to have to go hunting.

Chapter 36

After more than an hour of prowling the alleys and looking into saloons, Longarm found no sign of Timothy Wright's brother. Nor of anyone else wandering the streets with a shotgun and a grudge.

Al Gray would have killed him without a qualm and laughed about it afterward. But Gray was not in town. Longarm was confident that marshal Wilson Hughes would tell him when Gray did return; the man wanted that second hundred-dollar payout that Longarm had promised.

He sometimes wondered just what it was that the marshal thought Longarm wanted with Gray. Something far beyond the law to be sure, but Longarm had never said exactly what it was that he had in mind. And did not intend to.

For the moment, though, it was the Wright brother he wanted to lay hands on.

If he found the son of a bitch—*when* he found the son of a bitch—Longarm intended to beat the shit out of him and then break that shotgun. Preferably by smashing it over the man's head.

But first he needed to find Wright, and that was proving to be more difficult than it seemed.

Eventually he decided that Wright must have fled the city. His ambush attempt failed and he surely knew that Longarm would be hunting him, so it was logical that he would run away. After all, he was not really a gunman. A miner, perhaps, but not a gunman.

After being shot at Longarm was in no mood for a night on the town. Besides, some of the shot pellets that Wright fired at him had struck thin cloth as well as the stiff tweed that he favored, and his belly felt a little itchy. He suspected some of those pellets had gotten through to his flesh.

He stopped at an apothecary for some bandage cloths and a small bottle of alcohol, changed his mind, and went next to a saloon and bought a bottle of rye whiskey. After all, it had alcohol in it, too, and unlike wood alcohol intended for medicinal use, after he was done using it outside the skin he could pour some inside, too.

Longarm carried his purchases back to his hotel and upstairs to his room.

The door to the room stood slightly ajar.

It was not impossible that Wright and his shotgun could be inside.

Longarm transferred his bandages and the bottle of rye to his left arm and palmed his .45.

If someone was in there, the son of a bitch was as good as dead, for Longarm was in no mood to be fucked with.

He took a deep breath.

And kicked the door open.

Chapter 37

"You startled me," Melody Thompson said. The lady was lying in Longarm's bed. She was, he noticed, rather completely—and prettily—naked.

Longarm grinned. "Now that's somethin' to come home to," he said.

He walked into the room, shoved his .45 back into the leather, and closed the door. He reached up and shot the bolt closed to lock it behind him.

He deposited his purchases on the bedside table, leaned down, and gave Melody a long, lingering kiss.

"You smell nice," he said.

"You don't," Melody accused him. "You smell like a goat. Get naked so I can give you a bath."

"Now that's the nicest thing anybody's said to me all day," Longarm told her. But he started pulling his clothes off, as instructed.

When he removed his shirt, Melody let out a subdued shriek. "Custis, what are those wounds?"

"Uh, shotgun pellets," he said. "I had a little problem a little while ago."

"That is terrible. Let me take care of those. Lie down here. Do you have any bandages?"

He pointed to the paper wrapped package on the table. "Bandages an' antiseptic, too. That's what I got 'em for."

Melody changed places with him and opened the package of bandage cloth. She tore off a small piece and soaked it with whiskey, then carefully cleaned the blood away from the punctures on his stomach.

She felt each wound to make sure there was no lead still inside and found two where the pellets were embedded. "Do you have a knife? I need to dig these out." She laughed. "No, don't look at me like that. They're really just superficial, but I don't want to leave them in. Now tell me, where is your knife?"

Longarm pointed to his trousers, lying on the seat of his chair. Melody retrieved Longarm's pocketknife, opened it, and wiped the alcohol-laden cloth over the blade before she bent close and very gently probed each of the two wounds until she was able to extract the lead pellets.

"You act like you done this before," Longarm observed.

"That is because I have. Never mind where or for who," she said, still concentrating on the five small punctures in his stomach. Finally she stood. "Good. That seems to be everything."

She wet the cloth with more rye and carefully swabbed each puncture, then got the roll of cotton bandage. "Sit up," she said. "I need to be able to wind this around you. There, that's better."

She wound the bandage tightly, taking four wraps around

his midsection to cover all the punctures, then tied the bandage off.

"You do nice work, Nurse Thompson," he said.

"There is one more thing you need," Melody told him.

"An' what would that be?"

"Lie down again. I need to drain your balls."

"Ah. Sounds like an excellent plan. Very restorative."
Longarm laughed. He lay down, his pecker standing tall.

Melody bent over him again. But this time her nursing had nothing to do with wounds. She peeled back his foreskin, leaned down lower, and opened her pretty mouth.

Chapter 38

Longarm woke before dawn, as was his habit. Melody lay snuggled close and warm at his side. He dimly remembered her getting up in the night and using the thunder mug after fumbling around for it and moving his trousers out of her way.

He rolled onto his side and pulled Melody to him so that their bodies fit together like spoons.

Longarm's morning hard-on poking her in the ass roused Melody, and she smiled and shoved her butt back against him. She lifted her leg to allow him entry to her pussy, and he lay there, socketed deep inside the warmth of her body.

He placed one arm across her body and cupped her right tit in his hand. It was warm and soft, her nipple hard against his palm.

"Nice," she whispered.

Melody smelled of flowers and yeast and dried sweat. It was not an unpleasant combination.

Neither of them moved for a time. Then very slowly and

softly he began to stroke in and out. She responded by pushing back against him.

After a few minutes Melody's breathing quickened, and he could feel her pussy clenching and fluttering against his cock. She gave a tiny, subdued cry as she reached a climax.

Longarm began to move faster then, driving harder and deeper until he was pummeling her ass with his belly. And ramming her cunt with his hard cock.

He reached his own climax, spewing jism inside Melody's body.

"Ow, that hurts," Melody said.

"Too deep?"

"Your hand on my tit. You're hurting me."

"Sorry." He had not realized that when he came he clutched her breast so very hard. "Should I kiss it and make it well?"

Melody laughed. "No, but stay inside me for a while, will you, please? It feels nice there." She pressed her butt back against him. Her thighs trapped his cock where it was, but he certainly did not mind that.

In a few minutes her breathing steadied and slowed down, and she dropped off to sleep again.

Longarm lay where he was, enjoying the feel of her slender body warm against his.

After a little while he dozed, too, still locked inside Melody's pussy.

Chapter 39

"Breakfast?" he asked when the two of them were dressing after finally getting out of bed.

Melody smiled. "Spending time with a gentleman outside the bedroom. Imagine that."

"Is that a yes or a no?" he asked.

"Oh, it is a yes." She curtsied. Or tried to. The effect was imperfect considering that Melody was still naked at the time. "I would be pleased to accompany you to breakfast, sir."

Longarm kissed her. "Good."

"Careful now. You'll get something started again." Melody laughed. They had made the beast with two backs again when they awakened this time. Longarm was not sure, but he suspected most of the morning was past. Not that he regretted the time spent in bed with Melody Thompson. Far from it. It was time delightfully spent. The girl was a marvel of energy in bed.

They washed and finished dressing and he extended his arm to escort her out.

"La," she said. "Such a gentleman." Then Melody became serious. "Are you sure you won't mind being seen with me in public, Custis? I'm not welcome in polite society, you know."

Longarm smiled. "You're always welcome with me, dar."

Melody rose onto tiptoes and kissed the side of his neck.

"Careful," he said, "or you'll get somethin' started."

Melody laughed. "Lead on then."

Longarm squired her downstairs and out onto the street. As he had suspected, it was late morning and the town was busy.

They went down the street to Buck Walters's café where half a dozen men were having midmorning coffee. Longarm led Melody to an empty table and held the chair for her to sit. He chose a spot so he could face the doorway—an old habit that had saved his life more than once—then walked over to the counter.

"We'll have two o' your good breakfasts, Buck, if you're still serving," he said.

"Coming right up, Custis."

Buck's wife, who had never uttered a word to Longarm in the time he had been coming here, glanced across the room, then left her stove for a moment to come around the end of the counter and lean in close to Longarm.

She whispered, "Could be you don't know this, but that pretty girl you are with . . . she is no lady."

Longarm pretended not to understand Mrs. Walters's meaning. "I'm sorry, uh, how d' you mean that?"

Mrs. Walters came even closer and motioned him to lean down. She put her mouth practically in his ear and said, "She is a hoor, that's what she is."

"A hoor? Are you sure?"

"Oh, yes. I mean . . . all the ladies . . . I mean I've never actually . . . never mind then."

"Thank you for telling me that," he said, his tone and expression serious. But he was laughing silently to himself when he headed back to the table.

At least Buck, that good and generous man, was willing to serve them. Longarm knew there would be places in town where they could not have gotten service. In the saloons, yes. But in more respectable establishments, service could have been in doubt.

When he got back to the table he said, "I asked for breakfasts though I suppose it's closer to lunchtime than breakfast. Is that all right?"

"Fine," Melody said.

Longarm sat, relaxed and comfortable. And quite thoroughly drained to the point that there was a dull ache down in the region of his empty balls.

Chapter 40

"Can I ask you something, Custis?" Melody asked, leaning forward and placing her hand on top of his.

"O' course," he said.

"Tell me all about yourself," she said. "I want to know everything. Who you are. Where you come from. What you do for a living."

Longarm smiled. "Well, little darlin', I'm nothing special. Just the fella you see here. I come from West by God Virginia. But that was a long time ago. Since then I drifted some. Did a little o' this and a lot o' that. As for how I make my money"—he grinned—"folks just kinda give it to me."

And that was the truth. The taxpayers of the United States did indeed just give it to him. In exchange for certain services that he did not want Melody Thompson or anyone else in Crowell City to know about.

"There is more to you than that," Melody said. "I can sense that about you. Usually I am very good at reading people . . . for a while I even worked in a traveling show. I was a fortune-teller." She laughed. "I wore a turban and silk robe and everything. It was fun while it lasted. Then the show fell apart, and I was left on my own with no money, no family . . . they had disowned me long since. So I became what I am today." She laughed. "The money is better now anyway."

"Money," Longarm said. "You haven't mentioned a word to me about money."

"That is because you are special. And because I can't read you like I can most men," Melody said. "So I am curious about you. I want to know everything."

Longarm shrugged. "You already know everythin' worth knowin'."

Melody opened her mouth to speak, but she was interrupted by the arrival of their plates.

Later, after they had eaten a most pleasant breakfast, Longarm stood and reached into his pocket to pay.

There was something not quite right. It took him a moment to realize what that something was.

The bills in his pants pocket were not arranged the way he normally carried them. His habit was to fold any paper currency and shove it into his pocket with the "closed" end of the fold pointing down. Now his bills were placed so that the "open" end was down and the closed end pointing up.

Melody had moved his trousers in the night. Or so he thought at the time. It seemed she had also been going through his pockets.

Helping herself perhaps? He would have to count his money to be sure, but it certainly felt like everything was there.

"Excuse me, darlin'. I'll go pay Buck for our meals."

He went to the counter and pulled out his wad. Flipped quickly through it.

Every cent was where it had been. Melody had taken nothing.

But he knew now that she had been going through his pockets. He probably interrupted her when he woke up. He could not remember if he spoke to her then, but he distinctly recalled having wakened when she got up to take a piss.

Longarm returned to the table they had shared, pulled out her chair, and again offered his arm to escort her out onto the streets of Crowell City.

He wondered as they walked though: Just what the hell was Melody's game?

Chapter 41

"Oh, I'm not going back to the hotel, if you don't mind," Melody said. "I have some things to do. Could you walk me over to Harriman's Livery, please?"

"If you'll tell me the way," Longarm told her.

Melody held on to his arm as they walked to the edge of town and into the ramshackle barn. The corrals were mostly empty except for a few burros standing in the shade. "Hello, Harry," she said, smiling at the hostler.

Harry obviously had suffered severe burns at some point in the past. The entire left side of his face was shiny, red flesh. His left eye was a white, opaque ball resting beneath a brow that had no eyebrow hair at all.

"The buggy, Miss Thompson?" Harry asked.

"Please."

"Yes'm." Harry turned and hurried away.

Melody smiled up at Longarm. "Harry is a dear man," she said. "I let him fuck me in exchange for the use of his horse and rig." She laughed. "Don't look so shocked, dear. I am a whore, after all. Fucking is what I do for a living."

"Y'know, I almost forgot that," Longarm said.

"Harry mostly keeps burros. He rents them out to the mines. Apparently it is a very profitable business. Well, not very profitable perhaps, but there is profit enough. Harry has very simple needs."

When the man returned he was leading a handsome gray pulling a small opera coach. The cab was completely enclosed with the driving lines extending from the horse's bit through a cutout in the dashboard.

"Here you go, Miss Thompson."

Longarm helped Melody into the coach while Harry made sure all the straps and buckles were correct. Then both men stepped back while Melody drove away.

"Nice lady," Harry observed.

"Ayuh," Longarm said. "Does she do this often?"

"Take that rig? Oh, yes. Every few days she goes for a drive. I don't know exactly where she goes. Probably out along the creek. You know, just getting away from folks for a little while. She doesn't seem to have any lady friends. The upper crust won't have anything to do with her, and the lower sort of working girl think she is snooty."

Harry turned his head and spat. "I know better. Those girls in the saloons won't have me. It's because of what I look like. I'm an ugly man. I know that. But Miss Thompson doesn't seem to see that. She acts toward me like I'm normal. And her such a beautiful woman." He sighed. "I love her for that."

"It was good t' meet you, Harry." Longarm extended his hand to the man, then headed back into town.

Chapter 42

Longarm was having a drink in one of the town's many saloons when Wilson Hughes sidled up to him.

"I just thought I would let you know. No news recent about your, um, friend," the town marshal said. "But I expect some soon."

"All right, thanks."

"Buy me a drink?"

Longarm did not like the man but it would have been rude to refuse. He knew good and well that Hughes could afford to buy his own drinks. After all, Longarm had already paid him more than a hundred dollars in bribes. And promised more after that.

Longarm nodded to the barman, who brought Hughes a beer and a shot. The bartender extracted the price of Hughes's drinks from the change lying in front of Longarm.

"What d'you know about Melody Thompson?" Longarm asked. The marshal seemd to be Crowell City's most complete source of information, and if he had to drink with the man he might as well get some good out of the experience.

"Other than the fact that she sells pussy for a living?" Hughes asked, snickering.

"Yeah, I already got that much," Longarm said.

"I'm not real sure I can remember anything," Hughes said, taking a sip from his shot and following the raw whiskey with a swig of beer.

Longarm sighed. Reached into his pocket and extracted a twenty-dollar double eagle, which he slid across the bar to Hughes.

Hughes smiled as he pocketed the coin. "What do you want to know?" he asked.

"Who she is," Longarm said. "She doesn't act like a normal whore. That is, I know that she is one. But something about the woman doesn't quite ring true." He took a drink of his rye. "Am I making any sense here, Wilse?"

"I think so. You are right that she is not your usual sort of working girl. For one thing, she has a boyfriend. The man is not a pimp. In fact, he might be her legal husband." Hughes's smile was sly. He took another drink.

"It isn't generally known," the marshal said, "but they work together in some ways, I think. You, uh, you know the man, or anyway know about him."

"I do?" Longarm was genuinely puzzled by the comment. "Who the hell are you talkin' about?"

Hughes laughed. "Your pal Al Gray, that's who."

"Melody? And Gray? Well, I'll be a son of a bitch."

Hughes's laughter became louder until Longarm thought he might choke on his own amusement. Which was, in fact, a rather pleasant thought. *Choke on your own puke, cocksucker.*

He was surprised but now understood why Melody
Thompson was snuggling up to him. And asking questions.
After all, he made no secret of the fact that he was here hoping to meet Gray and speak with him about some unspeci-
fied something.

That would explain too why she had gone through his
pockets during the night but did not take anything. She did
not want money; she wanted information. He tried to
remember where he had put his badge and if she might have
found it in her nocturnal search.

The badge and wallet were hidden beneath the mattress
in his room, and he was fairly sure she could not have
reached that without disturbing his sleep.

He thought he had shoved it under the mattress far
enough that she would have difficulty reaching it and would
almost have to know where it was in order to find it.

So he was safe.

Probably.

He was still hoping that Gray would present himself, thinking to meet someone who had a line on something illegal but
lucrative. And wouldn't the bastard be surprised to see Longarm standing there ready to take him back into custody.

Longarm wanted Gray and had not forgotten the rifleman
who came so close to killing him out there on the trail.
Bringing in the two of them would be a great joy.

As for Melody . . . he did not know what to think or to
do about her.

He would cross that bridge when he came to it.

"Have another drink, Wilse," he said, tossing back the
rest of his whiskey and lifting a finger to call for another.

Chapter 43

The barber had an easy way with scissors and razor. Longarm leaned back in the articulated chair and closed his eyes.
The sounds of the barbershop surrounded and lulled him.
The low hum of conversation from others waiting their
turn—or simply loafing in the shop—the slap of the strop
and the click of the scissors. It was a relaxing experience.

Then his pleasant reverie was interrupted when he heard
one of the loafers say, "Oh, shit!"

Longarm's eyes snapped open to see a man silhouetted
against the bright sunlight at the doorway. The only thing
he could make out was that the fellow was carrying something long. A shotgun?

Longarm sat upright, ignoring the barber, who had a
razor at his throat.

His lap was covered with the striped cloth intended to
catch falling hair.

"You!" the fool with the shotgun said.

"Is that you, Wright?" Longarm asked, the entire right side of his face covered with lather.

"It's me all right, you son of a bitch," Timothy Wright's brother snarled.

He stepped forward, into the shadowed interior of the barbershop, and Longarm could properly see him. Wright looked pleased with himself. He glanced toward the side wall where a row of pegs held Longarm's coat and hat along with a number of others. And where there were four gun belts hanging as well.

The expression on Wright's face broadened to a wide smile. "Don't have your damn pistol now, do you, fucker? You remember. The gun you used to murder my brother."

"Can I ask you something, Wright?" Longarm said, motioning for the barber to step aside.

"I got you dead to rights, Long, so go ahead and ask. I ain't in no hurry to send you to hell," the fellow said.

His shotgun was cocked, Longarm saw, ready to fire at the touch of a trigger.

"What's your name?" Longarm asked.

Wright looked puzzled. "I thought you knowed that. It's Wright. You remember my brother? His name was Timothy. But he's gone now. Dead and buried, and you're responsible for that."

Longarm nodded. The loafers, he noticed, were staying put to see the show. They obviously expected blood. And they would get it.

"And your name?"

"Carl, mister. That's short for J. Carlisle Wright. I'm the last one of our family that's left. But one is all it takes to avenge Tim's murder."

"All right, Carl. I'll make sure the stone carver gets your

whole name on the marker over your grave. An' that's a promise from me t' you. I take promises serious. I'll see that it's done."

Carl Wright huffed and said, "That'd be nice except you're the one as is gonna die."

He started to tip the barrel of his shotgun up toward Longarm.

Longarm's .45 roared, blowing the sheet outward and setting it ablaze where his bullet passed through ahead of its lance of fire.

Carl Wright looked down at his chest, his expression incredulous. Then he glanced over toward the pegs and all the guns hanging against the wall.

"They aren't mine, Carl," Longarm said just as Wright dropped to his knees. And then forward onto his face.

His shotgun clattered hard on the floor, and Longarm flinched, fully expecting the impact to dislodge the hammer and fire the gun. Fortunately there was no discharge. He and the other men in the shop began to breathe easier.

"Rory, you'd best run over and fetch Marshal Hughes," the barber said.

"What about an undertaker?" Longarm asked.

"Oh, that's me." The man smiled. "At least this time I don't have to drag him far."

Chapter 44

Longarm allowed town marshal Wilson Hughes to take his .45—but neglected to mention the .44-caliber derringer he always carried in his vest pocket—and marched docilely in front of Hughes to the Crowell City jail.

When they were out of public view, Hughes dropped Longarm's Colt onto his desk, yawned, and pulled out a desk drawer. "Drink?"

"I could use one," Longarm said.

"All I have is bourbon. Is that all right?"

"I've always thought that any whiskey in hand is better'n some other brand elsewhere," Longarm said.

"Sit down then and we will . . . talk," Hughes said.

Longarm took the hint and dug a double eagle out of his pocket. He flipped it onto the desk and reached for the bottle.

"Huh-uh," Hughes said.

Longarm's hand stopped, his fingers curled around the neck of the whiskey bottle. "What's wrong?" he asked.

"What is *wrong*," Hughes said, "is that now you've killed two men in my town."

"Meaning?"

"Meaning the price has gone up. I'll want twice that to keep you out of jail until you see the magistrate."

"You're a hard man, Wilse, an' a thief." Longarm smiled. "And them's just two of the things I like about you." He found another gold coin in his pocket and added it to the one already lying on the desk.

Hughes picked up both and dropped them into his pocket. He smiled and said, "I'll let you know when to show up for your court hearing."

"You have a magistrate in town?" Longarm asked.

"No, but if we really need one they'll send Sam Carver over from the county seat," Hughes said.

Longarm grinned. "An' you'll tell me if Judge Carver happens by, won't you?"

"Count on it," Hughes said.

"Nothing new on your friend Gray?" Longarm asked.

"Not yet. Maybe when Melody gets back to town she'll know something more. She keeps up with his movements; I don't know how," Hughes said.

Then he gave Longarm a worried look. "You aren't forgetting our deal, are you? I mean, I let the cat out of the bag about her and him being friends. I wouldn't take it kindly if you was to make a separate deal with her."

Longarm grunted. But said nothing. The truth was that he would like to see Wilson Hughes fired from his town marshal's job and made to do some actual work for his livelihood. There was little Longarm detested more than a bent lawman, and Hughes was so far bent he could probably kiss his own ass.

He had another drink of Hughes's whiskey—Longarm preferred rye, but he was not a fanatic on the subject—he did not mind a drink of bourbon now and then.

"Thanks, Wilse. We'll talk more when Miss Thompson returns."

He picked up the dove-gray Stetson—he did sorely wish he could find another flat-crowned brown hat instead, but that would likely have to wait until he returned to Denver, hopefully with Gray and that sharpshooter in chains—and touched the brim in silent salute then headed back for the hotel to see if Melody was back yet.

Chapter 45

"Oh, shit!" Longarm said aloud. A passing matron turned and gave him a look of glaring disapproval.

He stopped where he was and tried to think. Melody Thompson certainly knew him. Knew his name but little else about him. She definitely did not know what his business was. No one in Crowell City knew that.

But Al Gray. Would he recognize Longarm's name?

Longarm could not recall for sure if he had introduced himself when he took the man into custody. And if he had, would Gray remember the name now, especially since as far as Alton Gray knew, the deputy who had been transporting him down to Denver was dead now, killed by that sharpshooter back in the mountain valley.

Not that there was anything Longarm could do about it at this late date. Melody was in contact with Gray somehow. Either she met him on her excursions away from town, sent him telegraphic messages, was in touch with him by whatever means.

If she mentioned Longarm by name and *if* Gray recognized the name, well, the game would be up in that case.

But he did not know if either or both of those things happened, and he was not going to abandon his hope of grabbing Gray the easy way here in town. Marshal Hughes believed Gray was coming back. Obviously Melody had told the marshal that her boyfriend would return. Longarm simply had to go ahead on that basis until or unless he learned different.

When, though. When would Gray come back?

He wondered if he should ask Melody that direct question the next time he saw her.

It probably would do no damage to do so. Hughes had undoubtedly already tipped her to the fact that Longarm was wanting to see Gray about something. She knew so why not bring it up to her? Lord knew they were on friendly enough terms.

Longarm cracked a smile, thinking about Melody. Thinking about that slim, sensuous, oh-so-enjoyable body of hers.

Just thinking about her gave him a hard-on.

The same pinch-mouthed old biddy who had been so disapproving of his language a moment earlier must have noticed the bulge rising in his trousers because this time she whirled around and practically ran in the other direction.

Must never have seen a cock before, Longarm thought, not at all distressed by the matron's shock and dismay.

With that happy thought in mind he tipped his Stetson to the lady, then turned and headed into the nearest saloon.

Chapter 46

The idea was that a low-life sort like he was playacting to be here in Crowell City would—and did—consort with fallen women. That was what people expected from the criminal sort, wasn't it?

And the little soiled dove at the back of the barroom was awfully pretty.

Longarm paused to question whether the girl really was that pretty . . . or whether it was the whiskey talking.

No, he decided, she really was that pretty. Probably hadn't been in the business long enough to get that hard outer veneer of contempt for her customers. It was his experience—and he had plenty of experience—that whores tended to develop those feelings after a while.

This one was hanging back a little, idling behind the billiards table while the other girls were out front, circulating among the customers and cadging drinks.

This girl looked fresh and friendly. And he could use a

friendly exchange. Pretending to be something he was not was not an easy task.

The brief time he spent in Wildwood with Bob Kane had been enough to remind him of that. It had been a great relief to be able to be himself with Bob, no pretenses, no posturing, no acting the criminal looking to make a connection with another of his kind.

Here . . .

Longarm tossed back his fourth . . . or fifth . . . or whatever whiskey and motioned for the girl to join him.

She was small. She reminded him of the girl in Wildwood. A little. She had black hair pulled back and done up in a tight bun, apple cheeks, and a small mouth. He looked at her lips and visualized them wrapped tight on his cock. The thought made his erection grow all the harder.

When she came closer he could see her eyes. They were pale gray and very bright.

"You're pretty," he said when she moved up against him and slipped her arm around his waist.

"Thank you, sir." She smiled. "My name is Hortense. And before you ask, yes, I am tense." She laughed. "Seems almost prophetic, doesn't it?"

"Prophetic?" he said.

"Look, mister, I'm a whore. That doesn't mean I'm stupid, just that I have to make my way in this world somehow and fucking is about all I know. I've been doing it since I was ten thanks to my uncle. I got tired of that and ran away from home. Okay?"

"I meant no offense," he said. "Really."

"If you're interested," Hortense said, "my pussy is still tight, and I give great head. It will cost you two dollars for half and half or a buck for one or the other. I'll give it an honest try, but if you're too drunk to come, I'll give up. All right? Interested?"

"How much for all night?" he asked.

"That would be ten dollars."

"Stiff," he said.

Hortense giggled. "So are you, honey." She reached down and placed her hand on the bulge in his trousers. "Do you have a room somewhere?"

"Uh-huh. Over at the hotel."

The girl linked her arm into his, looked up at him, and said, "What are we waiting for, honey?"

"I can't think of a single reason," Longarm said, leading her out onto the street.

On the way out the door he almost bumped into a fellow who was just coming in.

"Sorry," he said automatically. He was half a dozen paces down the sidewalk when it occurred to him that the new arrival had looked awfully familiar.

His thoughts were occupied with something more pressing, however, and he put the man out of mind.

Chapter 47

"Let me take care of you, honey," Hortense said when they were in Longarm's room with the door locked behind them. She moved in close and began unfastening his buttons and buckles. Took his clothing item by item and carefully hung or folded each and set them aside. While she worked she hummed a pleasant tune. Longarm tried to recall the title of the song; he knew he had heard it many times before but could not now remember what it was called.

No matter. It was soft and nice.

So was Hortense.

When she was naked she was even prettier than when clothed. He had run into a few women like that. Being without covering of any sort made them actually better looking.

Hortense's body was compact, almost athletic. She was lean and firm. Her tits were pale, small, and tall. They stood up proud and tip-tilted, her nipples so red he suspected she put rouge on them to achieve their color.

Her belly was flat above a dark bush that had been trimmed short. She had a tiny waist with a flare of hip below and a round little ass.

Hortense released her hair from the pins and shook her head. Her hair cascaded down over her shoulders and back, reaching almost down to that round, pretty ass.

"Do you like what you see?" she teased.

Longarm smiled and nodded. "I like."

She put her hands on his chest and moved him back to the bed. Sat him down there but stopped him from turning and lifting his legs onto the mattress.

"Not yet," she said as she dropped to her knees in front of him. She was smiling.

Hortense leaned forward, so close he could feel her breath on his cock as she examined it. She ran her fingertips up and down the length of him. Peeled his foreskin back to expose the dark red bulb of its head.

She lifted his balls on the fingers of one hand and with her other hand lightly tickled the sensitive flat that lay between his balls and his asshole. Longarm squirmed, so worked up that he thought he might squirt come onto both of them without ever entering her.

When he was sure he had neared the limits of his ability to hold back, Hortense took him into her mouth.

And he had been right when he saw her over in that saloon. Those lips looked just fine when they wrapped around his prick.

She sucked. Gently at first, then harder, deeper, her head bouncing up and down on his cock, driving herself down onto it and sucking hard when she pulled back.

More quickly than he would have thought possible, Longarm felt the gather and rise of his sap.

He cried out as his jism shot hard and hot into Hortense's throat.

The girl continued to suck until the last drops were out. Then she gently massaged his balls, ran her hands over his chest and belly, pressed him down onto the bed.

"Right," she said, sounding happy and eager. "Now that that is out of the way, you and I can get down to some real fun."

She moved onto the mattress and began licking his nipples, which had become unusually sensitive under Hortense's touch. Her tiny body felt like it weighed next to nothing, and her breath was hot on his moist skin where her tongue had passed.

While she licked him she slowly moved on top of him, straddling his body and spearing herself on his cock, taking him deep, deeper until he was fully inside her body, surrounding him with the heat of her flesh.

He began to move involuntarily, his hips rising to meet her movement, softly at first, then quicker, deeper, harder until their bellies were pounding and pummeling, smacking wet with a mingling of sweat and pussy juices, until the sensation became almost too much to bear and again his loins contracted in an upward spasm of his climax.

Hortense collapsed on top of him, her hair spread out over his chest, her legs on either side of his, his dick still inside her.

Longarm closed his eyes.

He smiled and lightly stroked the back of her head. He remembered the old saying "pretty is as pretty does." Little Hortense had it both ways, pretty to look at . . . and damned pretty in bed as well. It was not a bad combination.

He figured to rest a little, then see what else the girl could do.

Chapter 48

"Breakfast?" Longarm offered around dawn the next morning as he washed himself after he and Hortense had again made the beast with two backs.

She smiled and came onto tiptoe to kiss the side of his neck. "Thank you very much, but I got to get back to my kids."

"You have children?"

"Oh, yes. Two of them. They're the light of my life. Both of them boys. Two-year-old twins." She laughed. "They're a handful, let me tell you."

"But . . . uh . . ."

Hortense laughed again. "There is a lady who sits with them at night. Well, what it is, she sleeps in my place and watches the boys. The arrangement gives her a place to sleep and gives my kids someone to be there if they need anything. Now I'll go home and the sitter will leave, and I will give my kids something to eat." She smiled. "This ten dollars you gave me will feed us for the next two weeks."

"Shee-it," Longarm mumbled as he dug into his pocket and came up with a handful of change. He plucked a five-dollar gold piece out of the mix and handed it to her.

"Honey, I wasn't telling you all that to get a tip from you. You already paid me plenty."

"If I thought you was trying to sob-story me, I wouldn't have given you another dime," Longarm said. "All I want is for you t' take care o' those boys, all right?"

Hortense looked like she might break into tears. "You're a nice man, Mr. Long. Thank you." She sighed. "The truth is that I don't get many gentlemen. I'm not very pushy, and the other girls get most of the business. This money you gave me . . . it will go a long way toward taking care of all three of us."

"Good," he said. He kissed the top of her head and saw her to the door, then returned to the washstand and finished what he had been doing.

Day was just breaking when he went downstairs. Buck Walters had been open for business for some time and had eight customers already seated in the café when Longarm got there.

"Good morning, Long," Buck called from behind the counter. "I'll be with you in a minute."

"I'm in no rush," Longarm said, helping himself to a seat on one of the stools ranged along the front of the counter.

Someone had left a reasonably fresh Kansas City newspaper on the counter. Longarm picked it up and began perusing it. Among the articles in the newspaper was an account of a train robbery that had taken place sixteen days earlier. The mail car clerk and two passengers were killed. The robbers got away with an undisclosed amount of cash and mail from the safe. The Tatum gang was suspected.

Mail and the guard being involved made the robbery a federal crime.

Longarm knew the Tatums well. He had arrested the youngest of the Tatum brothers up in Wyoming two years earlier. The whole clan showed up for his trial on a charge of robbery from the mail. Young had gotten off with a fine and six months in confinement. Longarm had always wondered if the judge had been intimidated by the hard stares he received from the older brothers and their cousins the McCarthy boys.

Now they were involved in stealing from the mail again.

And Longarm was almost certain he had seen one of the brothers in the saloon the night before.

"Shit!" he said aloud. Of course. Last night. On his way out. The fellow he nearly ran into. That man had looked an awful lot like the middle Tatum brother, whose name was . . . Longarm had to dig through his memory to bring the name back to mind. Kurt, that was the name. Kurt Tatum.

And where there was one Tatum . . .

Chapter 49

There were three of them. Warren, Kurt, and Albert Tatum, he remembered. He had not thought about the Tatums in years, but now they were in the news. And apparently in Crowell City.

Bastards had killed an express car guard who was protecting the United States mail.

Their presence in town put Longarm in something of a quandary. He was trying to keep his identity as a deputy U.S. marshal quiet so as to bring Al Gray to him unsuspecting.

But the three Tatums trumped Al Gray, at least in Longarm's estimation. They killed an express guard. That made them wanted by the federal government. The deaths of the train passengers would be up to the state to prosecute. But the mail coach guard and theft of mail . . . that was up to Longarm and his fellow marshals.

If, that is, the man he saw last night was indeed Kurt Tatum.

Longarm had gotten only a glimpse of him, his main

attention being on Hortense. He could have been wrong. Perhaps the fellow was not Tatum after all.

If he was, though, if he and the rest of the clan really were here in Crowell City, it was Longarm's sworn duty to take them in. As for Al Gray, it was a matter of birds in the hand versus birds in the bush.

The subterfuge that he hoped to toll Gray in with would just have to go by the boards. There was no way he would allow the Tatums or any of their gang to go free. Not after killing a mail guard.

The Kansas City newspaper article had not specified who the guard worked for, but it was very likely that the man had been a postal clerk. And theft from the mail alone, even if no one had been killed, was enough to make the robbery a federal offense.

Longarm did not want town marshal Wilson Hughes or anyone else in Crowell City to know that he was a deputy marshal, but if he had a chance to take down the Tatums, he would do so. Al Gray would just have to wait his turn.

"Everything all right?" Buck asked as he delivered a plate of bacon, biscuits, and gravy. "You look awfully grim this morning."

Longarm looked up from his reverie. He nodded and managed a smile. "Sure, Buck. Everything's fine."

And it was. He had worked out what he should do if—big "if"—he should run into either the Tatums or Al Gray. Now all he had to do was carry through with that resolve.

"Just fine." He picked up his fork and dug into his breakfast with an appetite churned to a high pitch by all the acrobatics he and Hortense had performed through most of the night.

Chapter 50

"I got a question for you, Wilse," Longarm said to the crooked town marshal.

It had taken him until midmorning to track down the sometimes elusive Hughes. Now he was sitting in the marshal's office with a cup of truly terrible coffee.

"Care for a cigar, Wilse?" Longarm asked, pulling two cheroots out of his pocket.

"That's your question?" Hughes returned, taking one of the slender cigars and carefully cutting the tip off with a folding pocketknife.

Longarm bit the twist off his cheroot and spat it into his palm. "No, o' course not. The seegar is meant t' butter you up an' put you in a mood to cooperate."

"The other hundred you owe me will do that nicely," Hughes said. "You didn't need the cigar."

"Wilse, I don't owe you a damn thing unless you deliver for me. But there's no sign of Al nor idea of when he might show up. Or might not show, I suppose. No, what I got in

mind is something along the same line o' thinking but . . .
different. A little."

"How different?" Hughes asked.

"Different name," Longarm said. "Same result."

"You mean about the hundred?"

"Uh-huh." Longarm struck a match and held the flame
first to Hughes's cheroot and then to his own. When both
cigars were burning nicely he sat back and made a few
smoke rings, then said, "Last night I saw a fella that I think
I recognized. It didn't dawn on me till later, but I think it
might've been a man I'd seen a couple years back. Fella by
the name of Tatum. The last I heard he was runnin' with his
brothers. Good men, all of them. Salty, if you know what I
mean."

"I know the Tatum boys," Hughes said. "Them and me
have what you might call a business arrangement. Which,
come to think of it, you might want to consider for yourself.
If the law comes for you . . . and mind now, I'm not saying
that you are wanted anywhere . . . but if the law were to
come after you, I'd know about it, and I'd take care of it.
Keep you safe and out of sight until the danger blew over.
You know what I mean?"

Longarm blew some more smoke rings and nodded. "I
think I do, Wilse. An' you would do this for a, uh, a modest fee?"

"Very modest. Twenty dollars per month per man, and
you are safe from the law."

"I like that," Longarm said.

"I've never lost anyone yet," Hughes said modestly.

"Al Gray, for instance, or his sharpshooting friend," Longarm said.

"Or the Tatum boys or about a half dozen others I could name but won't."

"You're pulling in a tidy sum," Longarm observed.

"Yes, but for the parties involved it is money well spent. They get to walk free; I add to my retirement fund," Hughes said.

"And everybody is happy," Longarm said.

"Are you interested in meeting the Tatums?" Hughes asked.

Longarm nodded. "Ayuh, so I am. I could talk t' them about, well, about what I had intended for Gray."

"And I would get the hundred," Hughes said.

"That's right. You would get the hundred," Longarm agreed.

"Understand now, I can't speak for the Tatums, but they might be interested in listening to what you have to say," Hughes said.

"I understand that," Longarm agreed. "You get yours for setting up the meeting, not for them agreeing to anything, same as our deal with Gray had been."

"I tell you what then," Hughes said. "Meet me here this evening after dinner. Say, nine o'clock. Even with my protection the Tatums don't like to show themselves around town in daylight, but they like to socialize the same as any man. Come twilight they like to unwind, play a little poker, have a drink or maybe get laid, you know."

"Ayuh, I know how it can be." Longarm grinned. "Just this morning I was reading about why they might want t' be careful for a spell. Nine o'clock, you say? Here in your office?"

"Right," Hughes said. "I'm not making any promises on

their behalf, but I will talk to them and see if they would like to hear what you have to say."

"I can't ask fairer than that," Longarm told the man.

"And if they do agree to meet with you, I get the hundred," Hughes said.

"That's right. If this evening you tell me the Tatums will listen to what I say, then I'll pay you the hundred here in this office before we go an' meet them," Longarm said.

"Done," Hughes said.

"If they agree to the meet. Otherwise we go back to waiting on Gray and his partner." Longarm stuck his cheroot between his teeth and held out his hand to shake on the deal.

Chapter 51

Longarm was busy that afternoon. He was still torn, however. He wanted Al Gray and Gray's rifleman partner, the
one who had shot him and freed Gray. He wanted those two
bad. But at the same time he had his duty to perform, and
the Tatums were wanted on federal charges.

He would just have to take whichever he could get.

And toward that end, he had some shopping to do.

There was no gunsmith in Crowell City, but Anderson's
Hardware had a firearms section in the back. Longarm was
more than satisfied with his familiar, double-action Colt
.45. It felt like an old friend in his hand, but the cylinder
held only six shots.

If he came up against the Tatums this evening, he figured
there was a better than even chance that those three
brothers—and any gang members and hangers-on who happened to be with them—would resist being taken into
custody. He wanted more firepower than the .45 would
provide.

He bought a single-action Colt in the same .45 caliber as his tried-and-true model. The grips and the balance felt good in his hand, and it would give him another six rounds if he needed them. That revolver he stuck inside his waistband in the small of his back.

Much more importantly in the event there was trouble—and there very likely would be—he bought a break-top 12-gauge Stevens & Co. double-barrel shotgun. The gun was used but seemed to be in decent shape. The hammers came back with a smooth action, and the triggers pulled nicely as well. The bluing was worn away on both barrels, but he did not care about that.

The shotgun was a bargain at seven dollars and the revolver priced fairly at twenty-five. He bought ammunition for both, no. 2 goose shot for the shotgun and standard .45s for his revolvers. Longarm made sure to get a receipt to turn in to Henry when he got back to Denver.

Assuming he did get back to Denver.

From Anderson's he walked over to Dub Hilliard's smithy.

"Can you do a rush job for me this afternoon?" he asked the blacksmith. "I'll pay you well."

"Depends on what the job is," the wiry blacksmith said.

Longarm handed him the shotgun. "I need this cut down to, oh, eight inch or so barrels and braze or solder the rib between them. Can you do that for me before supper time?"

"I can," Hilliard said. "Hell, I can do it for you while you wait. It won't take but a few minutes." The man picked up a hacksaw and held out his hand for the gun.

Twenty minutes later Longarm had his sawed-off. Hilliard had done a good job of it, even taking a rat-tail file and smoothing the inside of the barrels where he had cut them.

"It's shiny, but you don't give me enough time to blue those spots," the smith apologized.

"It's just fine by me, and anybody lookin' at it from that end won't be complaining about the appearance," Longarm said.

He left the gun in his room and went down the hall to check on Melody—she was not in—then downstairs to eat.

He had some time to kill before his meeting with Wilson Hughes and, hopefully, with the Tatum brothers.

In the meantime he wondered if he could find Hortense for a little afternoon relaxation.

Chapter 52

Longarm responded to a light tapping on his hotel room door. He stepped to the side of the doorway and drew his Colt. It was not that he expected trouble but . . . just in case.

"Who is it?"

"It's me. Hortense."

Longarm slid the bolt back and opened the door. Hortense nervously eyed the revolver in his hand, then she said, "We need to talk. Can I come in?"

"O' course. Truth is, I was thinkin' about you earlier. Thinkin' about maybe asking you for a little afternoon delight."

"That would be fine, Mr. Long. You know I'll do anything you want. But first you have to listen to me for a minute," the girl said.

Longarm shut and locked the door behind her and motioned toward the bed. "Sit down an' tell me what brought you here."

"I don't mean to bother you but . . . a girl in my position hears things. If you know what I mean. And you are a nice man. You were good to me. You bought food for my kids.

You didn't have to pay me that much, but you did, out of the kindness of your heart you did."

Longarm retrieved a cheroot—the damn extra revolver dug hard into the small of his back—struck a match, and lighted it. Hortense surprised him by taking the slender cigar from him and starting to smoke it, so he pulled out another and lighted that one. He reminded himself to go buy more and hoped he could find a brand that he liked.

"The thing is," Hortense rambled on, "I heard you are being set up to be shot down."

Longarm's eyebrows went up at that information. Were the Tatums already aware that he was in town here and would be coming for them? Wilson Hughes could not have warned them. Hughes did not know that Longarm was a deputy marshal. The man would shit himself if he did find out. *When* he found out.

"She's an awful good shot, you know," Hortense was saying.

"She?" Longarm blurted.

"Yes. She used to be a sharpshooter in one of those traveling medicine shows before she hooked up with him. Now he robs some and pimps for her some and I don't know what all else."

"Now wait a minute," Longarm said. He did not know of any woman attached to the Tatum brothers, and they certainly were not in the business of pimping. "Who the hell are we talkin' about?"

Hortense gave him a look of disgust, as if saying he should pay attention. And perhaps he should at that. "Mr. Gray and Miss Melody, of course," the little whore said.

"I . . . Oh! Uh, tell me more about this, will ya?"

Chapter 53

"Tomorrow morning," Hortense said. "Marshal Hughes will come and tell you where you can find Mr. Gray. Except somewhere along the road, Miss Melody will be waiting to shoot you down." Hortense's brow furrowed. "I don't understand this, but she said something about you changing hats."

"Mel . . . say, how d' you know all this?" Longarm demanded.

"I eavesdrop sometimes." She giggled. "I eavesdrop a lot, actually. I heard Miss Melody talking to Marshal Hughes. To get him to do it, like. She, uh, she promised she'd give him a really good fuck if he does it. You wouldn't understand, but that is a powerful payment. None of the girls like to fuck Marshal Hughes, you see. He doesn't wash his cock, and it stinks. Absolutely nobody will suck him off, either. Especially that." Hortense shuddered, apparently just from thinking about it.

"Have you ever had to fuck him?" Longarm asked.

Hortense peered down toward her shoes. "Yes, sir," she

said in a very small voice. "I had to give it to him or go to jail. Whoring is against the law here, though you wouldn't know it the way folks act. Anyway, that is what the marshal does when he really wants some pussy. He grabs a girl and hauls her over to the jail. If she wants to get loose, she has to drop her knickers for him.

"I had to, you see, because my kids needed me. Otherwise I would have sat in their damn jail and let the town pay to feed me. But I didn't have that option, so I gave him the quickest fuck I could." She smiled up at him, her eyelashes long and curly against the pallor of her cheek. "Us girls know how to bring a man off fast if we want to or go the other direction and let him string it out. That would be like if we like a fellow. Or if we're enjoying it ourselves, which to tell you the truth doesn't happen very much."

"You're a nice girl, Hortense. Thank you for telling me all this," Longarm said. He slipped an arm around her waist and gave her a hug.

"Mr. Long."

"Yes, ma'am?"

"Would you, I mean . . . well, I like you just fine. And it would please me if we could get naked and, um, do stuff." She smiled. "Not for pay, you understand, but just because you're a boy and I'm a girl and . . . I like you."

Longarm smiled down at her. "As 't happens, I like you just fine, too, Hortense."

He stood and began unbuttoning his shirt.

Chapter 54

Hortense was soft in his arms and gentle. Longarm lay on his back and tried not to move while the girl nuzzled him and sighed.

She knelt over him and licked his nipples, first one and then the other. Her tongue roved lightly over his belly. Up and down the length of his cock. Down onto his balls and behind them to the sensitive flesh there.

"Roll over," she said.

"On my stomach?"

"Yes, of course on your stomach."

"What d' you . . . ?"

"Just do it," Hortense said.

With a shrug and a sigh, Longarm did as the girl asked.

He felt her leave the bed and turned his head to look. She had gone to the washstand beside the dressing table and was sloshing a washcloth in it. She seemed to be soaping the cloth.

When she returned to the bed she began washing Longarm's ass.

"That water is cold, y'know," he said.

"Are you complaining?"

"No. Just thought I'd mention it," he said with a grin.

"This won't take long."

"Good."

She washed him rather thoroughly, returned the washcloth to the washstand and fetched a towel, which she used to carefully dry Longarm's butt.

"I don't understand this," he said.

"Just mentioning again?"

"Yeah, something like that."

"Surely you've had anilingus before this?" Hortense said.

"I wouldn't know if I've had it or not since I don't know what it is," he admitted.

The girl laughed. And proceeded to lick his asshole.

"Damn if that don't feel awful good," Longarm said.

She lifted her head long enough to say, "It's supposed to, silly. Now let me get back to what I was doing."

She did. And it did indeed feel good. Different. But good. By the time Hortense sat up, Longarm's cock was about to explode.

He rolled over and smiled. "Now," he said, "it's my turn."

Chapter 55

Longarm treated himself to a thick steak sizzling in its own juices and a slab of apple pie for dessert. Then he went up to his room and retrieved the shotgun. Made sure it was loaded and checked the cylinders of both Colts, including the new one stuffed into the small of his back.

He always carried a few extra .45 cartridges, but now he took four shiny brass 12-gauge shotshells out of the box and dropped them into his coat pocket, too.

Then he went downstairs and walked over to the town marshal's office.

"You're early," Hughes said.

"Yeah," Longarm said, smiling. "I'm eager." He also wanted to avoid a setup like Melody and Gray seemed to be planning for the coming morning.

"Do you have my hundred?" Hughes asked.

"Right here." Longarm reached into his pocket and pulled out a wad of currency. He peeled off two fifties and placed them on the marshal's desk. "Paper be all right?"

"Fine," Hughes said. "Just fine." The bills disappeared into the man's pocket in the blink of an eye.

Hughes stood and reached for his hat. "Ready?"

"Been ready," Longarm said.

The marshal led Longarm down Crowell City's main street and left three blocks to the edge of town, where he opened the gate of a tall, neatly tended house.

"In here?" Longarm asked.

"Just knock. They're expecting you." He laughed. "They're expecting almost anyone. This is a whorehouse. The best we have. Beautiful girls. You'll see."

"You don't intend t' come in, do you?"

"Why, I had thought so. To introduce you around," Hughes said. "You boys don't know each other, and . . ."

"And you don't need t' be getting inta my business," Longarm said. "If it's all the same to you, I'd as leave you stayed out o' this."

"But I thought . . ."

"You been paid, Wilse. You done your good deed. Now go on back into town. If things go well, me and the Tatums will meet you later. Maybe all of us have a drink together." Or all meet in the marshal's office so Deputy U.S. Marshal Long could borrow the town's jail overnight. With Hughes in it, too, if he could think of a reason. "But right now," Longarm said to the crooked marshal, "I'm wantin' to keep our talk private."

"I . . . um . . . well." Hughes stammered and paused for a bit, obviously trying to think of a good reason why he should be included in the gang's discussions.

He could not, and in the end he turned and tugged his hat brim low and sulked his way back into town, shoulders slumped and boots shuffling in the dirt.

Longarm looked up at the big house and took a fresh grip on the sawed-off 12 gauge, then checked to make sure the spare pistol in his back was positioned so he could get to it in a hurry.

Then he took a deep breath and marched up the dirt pathway to the porch.

Chapter 56

His knock was answered by a dignified woman. He would not say she was elderly, but she certainly was bordering on it. She was dressed as if for a formal ball, with something sparkling woven into her graying hair and a gown, cut very low, that shimmered in the lamplight.

"Ma'am," he said, bowing slightly and making a leg.

The woman smiled. "Very nice, Mr. Long. Please come inside. Marshal Hughes said you wish to speak with some of my guests. You are entirely welcome to do so. If you require privacy"—she chuckled—"that is one of the things we do best."

"Thank you, ma'am," he said, handing his pale-gray Stetson to a young girl, either mulatto or Indian, who reached for it.

"One of your gentleman friends is in the parlor. Please join them. Josie will fetch you refreshment if you like. Just tell her what you want," the madam said.

"You're very kind." He smiled.

"May we, um, set that aside for safekeeping?" the woman asked, nodding toward his sawed-off.

"Actually, ma'am, I'd rather hang on to it, if you don't mind."

"And if I do mind?" she asked.

"Then I'd rather hang on to it."

The madam nodded to the mulatto girl, who bobbed her head and curtsied and hurried away with Longarm's hat.

"The parlor is through that doorway," the madam said, motioning to indicate a double-wide doorway.

"Thank you, ma'am."

Longarm stepped through the doorway and was confronted with a solid wall of perfume and powders. The place positively reeked of competing scents. It was filled also with beauty.

Four utterly gorgeous whores were seated on the gilded furnishings.

A gentleman Longarm had seen in the Crowell City bank was at the far end of the room with a stunning blond girl curled up in his lap.

And Warren Tatum was sitting in an overstuffed armchair to the left of the doorway.

Tatum saw Longarm about the same time that Longarm spotted him. "You, you son of a bitch!" he barked, reaching for his pistol.

Longarm tipped his shotgun up and tripped the front trigger. Warren Tatum's chest crumpled in on itself in a red mush. The room was filled with noise and smoke.

There was no need to fire the second barrel.

The girls squealed and screamed and fled from the room in a mad crush of velvet and satin. The banker took a look at Longarm and turned pale. He did not move.

Longarm stepped to the side and pressed against the wall while he broke the action of the scattergun, extracted the spent shell and shoved in a fresh one.

He peered around the edge of the doorway. True to form, the guests had the good sense to get the hell out of there. Probably, he thought, they were less worried about what he might do than they were about being caught up in a public spectacle and their wives finding out where they were spending their evenings.

The girls scattered first. But then they were not encumbered much by clothing. Darn good-looking girls though. Whoever owned this house had quite a stable of fillies.

Two men wearing shirts and underpants and carrying assorted other articles of clothing came next, followed by a large man with flaming red hair and a cigar stuck jauntily between his teeth.

Longarm stepped into view. "Stop right there, Albert," he snapped.

"Fuck you, Long." The big man reached for his pistol, but Longarm's 12-gauge was quicker.

Smoke and flame filled the foyer. Albert Tatum's left leg buckled but he was able to remain upright. He dragged his revolver out of the leather and struggled to cock it.

Longarm fired his second barrel. This time the load of heavy shot hit him in the belly and nearly tore the man in two. Albert Tatum tumbled head over heels down the staircase.

"Shit," Longarm mumbled. "Looks like I gotta dig the last one out."

He tossed the empty shotgun aside and pulled his spare Colt out of the small of his back, then started warily up the steps.

Kurt Tatum was in one of those rooms on the second floor, and by now he knew something was up.

Longarm held his Colt cocked and ready. He felt a flutter of apprehension in his belly, but this was something that had to be done.

Chapter 57

"Come on out, Kurt. We got you surrounded," Longarm shouted.

Most of the doors to the cribs along the hall were standing open after the occupants fled. Two remained closed. Longarm figured Kurt Tatum pretty much had to be inside one of those.

Temporarily. Longarm intended to have his ass out of there in another minute or two.

He stood in front of the first of the closed doors, hesitated for only a moment, then kicked the door open. Wood splintered and the latch was broken, and inside there were screams. Apparently this was the place where a number of the whores had taken refuge.

But there was no sign of Kurt.

Longarm touched the brim of his Stetson and nodded. "Sorry, ladies."

He moved down to the last closed door.

"Kurt. I'm takin' you in. The question is, d' you walk out or are you carried by your pallbearers," Longarm shouted.

A bullet came smashing through the flimsy door.

"Well," Longarm murmured, "that answers that question. Now I know where the bastard is."

He heard a crash from inside the room, followed by screams from the room next door.

With a grunt of effort, Longarm kicked the last door open, stepped into the doorway and triggered six quick shots from his "spare" .45, then dropped it and palmed his own tried and true Colt.

As he had more than half hoped, Kurt Tatum counted the shots and made the fatal mistake of thinking Longarm's gun was empty.

The man stepped into the hallway, emerging from the room next door after smashing through the paper-thin wall. He held a Remington revolver and wore nothing but a smirk as he prepared to gun down the lawman.

But instead of facing a man with an empty revolver, he looked into the muzzle of Longarm's Colt.

The .45 erupted, spewing lead and flame and smoke, all three of which flashed in the direction of Kurt Tatum's gut.

Longarm's first shot struck hard. The second doubled him over. A third, aimed with care, drove through Kurt's forehead and beyond. Tatum dropped as if he were poleaxed. He never got a shot off.

It took a few minutes for the smoke to clear and for people's hearing to return after the concussion of the gunfire indoors, but eventually heads began to appear inquisitively as the working girls came to look at the rivers of blood that had been spilled in their house.

"Someone best run get Marshal Hughes," Longarm said.

"I already sent my maid to fetch him," the madam responded. "Would you like a drink?"

"I would, come t' think of it," Longarm said. He had a headache from the repeated explosions, but it was nothing that a shot of rye could not cure.

"Go on into the parlor then," the madam told him. "There are decanters on the sideboard. Help yourself. Are you . . . that is to say . . . ?"

"No," Longarm said, even though he knew good and well that the woman was asking if he was the law. "Just bad blood." Which was true enough in a way. Those three had taken the life of a federal officer when they gunned down that mail clerk. That was more than enough cause for there to be bad blood between them.

Longarm got his drink. And his arrest. "We couldn't come to an agreement," he said when Marshal Hughes showed up.

He grinned when they got back to the jail. "How much is it gonna cost me this time t' bond out, Wilse?"

Chapter 58

Longarm was up early the next morning. Instead of going to Buck's café for breakfast he walked down to the livery and paid for a horse and saddle, then tied them on the street in front of the hotel before leaving the horse behind and walking to the café for a quick meal.

From there he hurried back to his room and sat at the window watching down the street to the town marshal's office. Melody Thompson showed up about eight thirty.

If the information Hortense gave him was correct, Melody would tell Hughes to wait a bit before he informed Longarm of Al Gray's supposed whereabouts. By then she would be in position to ambush him on his way to wherever that was supposed to be.

She was, he noticed, wearing riding clothes instead of her usual gown.

When she left the marshal's office, Longarm followed her, keeping well back and leading the rented horse.

The presence of the horse was actually a help to him and

not a bother. He could walk beside the animal and use it to shield him from view if she happened to turn and look around.

The woman's confidence was such that she never bothered to look behind her, though.

Melody went to a small house on the edge of town and went inside.

Longarm loitered behind a tall, spreading lavender bush, his horse cropping grass beside him, while Melody was inside. Five minutes or so after she went indoors she reappeared. And this time Al Gray was with her.

So was a long, fringed buckskin rifle scabbard. So far everything Hortense had said was right on the money. Longarm mouthed a silent thank-you to the little girl with the big heart. When he got back to town, he thought, he wanted to give that girl and her children whatever reward was posted for Gray. It seemed only fair.

As for Wilson Hughes, Longarm simply did not know what to do. He knew perfectly well what he *wanted* to do. He wanted to throw the son of a bitch behind bars.

But Hughes so far had done nothing that was against federal law. If Hughes had indeed sent Longarm on the trail where Al Gray and Melody Thompson would be waiting to kill him, Longarm could have arrested the man on a charge of conspiring to murder a federal officer. By bypassing that and following the lethal duo on his own, Longarm would not have that meeting with the marshal and so he could not prove the conspiracy.

It seemed a shame, he thought.

On the other hand . . .

Melody and Gray acted like they did not have a care in the world. Certainly they did not worry about anyone trailing them. They rode side by side, holding hands like a pair of lovers, on the road toward Wildwood, Gray astride and Melody on a sidesaddle. As if she were a virgin and needed to protect that cherry.

Custis Long kept out of sight as much as he could and followed.

The pair turned off the road two miles or so out of town and rode into an aspen grove on a low hill flanking the road.

Longarm's smile was grim as he looked for a place to leave his horse.

He intended to give them a little time up there—perhaps they could find some way to pass the time together while they waited for the fly to enter their trap—then, well, then they would just have to see who did what to whom.

Chapter 59

Fucking amateurs, Longarm thought. He had been over this road, back and forth, just days earlier and he could think of at least two other ambush sites that would have been better. Not that he was complaining.

They had chosen the place closest to town. Lazy bastards. Did they think he would be that easy to take down?

Longarm grunted softly to himself. Apparently yes, they indeed did think he was that easy. Hell, he had been the last time. Melody's bullet had missed by less than an inch that time or he would now be dead.

But then the last time he had not been expecting to be gunned down from ambush.

The difference was that this time he knew what he was up against.

He tied the rented horse—it was a good thing that the creature was a lazy, stumbling bum; it would not likely jerk free and run home—but took the stubby little shotgun with him.

He had four spare shotgun shells in his coat pocket, each of them loaded with a full ounce of no. 2 goose shot, and his two .45 Colts. He had thought about borrowing a rifle from Wilson Hughes, but that would have given the game away too soon. Hughes might well have found a way to warn Gray and Thompson about what Longarm was up to. It was a risk he did not need to take.

He checked the loads in his guns, stuffed the spare Colt into his waist at the small of his back, and began stalking the deadly duo.

There was no brush close beside the public road, but there was more than enough scrub oak and fans of spreading juniper on the string of low hills—mounds, really—on the side of the road where Gray and Melody were hiding.

Keeping out of sight from them as much as possible, Longarm took his time with the approach.

Whether deer or man, there is no trick to stalking them. Just take your time, think about how slowly you need to go and then go even slower. And watch where you put your clumsy damn feet. Of those, going slowly is the most important.

And Longarm did go slowly.

A tortoise could have outrun him, and he would not have minded in the slightest. He was careful to avoid letting the brush snag his clothing and even more careful about placing his feet where they would make the least noise.

They did make some noise. That was unavoidable. And in his ears those very faint cracklings of dried leaves sounded like drums pounding or signal guns booming.

Neither Al Gray nor Melody Thompson heard any of it.

He was able to creep up onto the hill behind them and then descend, slowly and carefully, until he was within nine or ten yards and at their backs.

Al Gray was the one who seemed to be nervous. Gray fidgeted. Picked a scab on his hand. Dug a fingernail into his ear. Stood up every minute or two to look back along the road Longarm was supposed to be following.

Melody was calm and businesslike. She had swept the leaves and twigs away to make a nest in the grass and stretched out there with the rifle beside her. She placed a low pile of flat rocks in front of her and padded them with a blanket she removed from behind her saddle. With a good rest to shoot from, he had no doubt she would be able to clip the ears off a housefly.

Her rifle was a custom outfit. A Schuetzen with double-set triggers, hooded sights, an odd-shaped stock, and a palm rest. He had no idea what the caliber would be. That could be a custom job as well.

Whatever, the rifle was a thing of beauty. Some gun maker somewhere should be justifiably proud of his creation despite the low purpose Melody was putting it to these days.

Longarm took a deep breath and dried his palms on his trousers, then stepped out of the brush behind and slightly above the two.

"Afternoon," he said cheerfully. "Nice day for a walk, ain't it?"

GIANT-SIZED ADVENTURE FROM
AVENGING ANGEL LONGARM.

BY TABOR EVANS

penguin.com/actionwesterns

M456AS0812

up like that. Now in a minute I'm gonna toss you some hand-cuffs. Melody, you can put 'em on your partner there."

Longarm held the shotgun aimed generally downhill while he dug in a pocket looking for some handcuffs.

"You son of a bitch," Melody snapped. "You changed hats. That's why I didn't recognize you. You were wearing a brown hat when I shot you. But I swear I thought I'd killed you. Now you have on that gray hat, damn you. How's come I didn't kill you that day?"

"Yeah," Gray said. "I saw you on the ground. I thought you were dead."

"Close," Longarm said, "but no cigar." He did not particularly feel like complimenting Melody on her marksmanship or telling her how very close she did come to killing him. "What was the deal there? Freeing your partner, were you?"

"At least that worked," Melody said.

"For a little while," Longarm agreed.

"You bastard," Melody snarled.

"Now, darlin', that's not the way you were talking to me the other night. You were cooing like a lovebird when you had my dick in you," Longarm said with a sarcastic smile.

"What!" Al Gray exploded. "You fucked him? You told me you didn't do anything with him."

"Oh, close your yap, Alton. I'm a whore. What would you expect me to do with him?" she returned.

"But the son of a bitch is a marshal. He's taking us to prison. And you, you bitch, you fucked him. If that wasn't bad enough, you lied to me about it afterward."

"At least he's a complete man, Al. You can't even get it up to fuck me," Melody said, contempt twisting her features.

"You bitch!" Gray dipped his hand into a pocket and came up with a tiny .22-caliber revolver. He pushed his hand forward. Pressed the little gun beneath Melody's left tit and pulled the trigger.

The explosion, small to begin with, was almost completely muffled by her flesh.

Melody looked down at herself, aghast, and fell.

Longarm's shotgun exploded and the left side of Al Gray's hip and belly were turned into red mush. Worse, one or more of the pellets ripped his stomach open. Gray coils of intestine spilled out.

The man collapsed. He fell on top of Melody, the coils of gut covering her pretty face.

By the time Longarm reached them Gray was dead. He pulled the man away from Melody and swept the shiny, gray coils off of her.

"At least," she whispered, "you won't get me into no damn courtroom to be stared at like a monkey in a cage. So fuck you, Long."

Longarm cleaned her up as best he could and sat with her until she was dead. Then he marked the spot so it could be easily seen from the road below. He found their horses and rode down to where he had left his animal.

The liveryman was going to be unhappy, Longarm knew, when he reclaimed the Remount Service's borrowed horses. And the gear that had been on them.

Hortense, on the other hand, should be pleased with the reward Longarm intended to see that she got. The money would go a long way toward taking care of her children.

As for that bastard Wilson Hughes, there was nothing Longarm could do about him. Longarm had no authority

when it came to state law. But oh, he wished he could come up with some federal charge against the man.

He intended to ask Billy Vail to look into that when he got back to Denver.

Which would not be soon enough.

Watch for

LONGARM AND THE WHISKEY RUNNERS

the 432nd novel in the exciting LONGARM
series from Jove

Coming in November!

Chapter 60

They looked to him like they nearly shit their pants at the sound behind them. Both rolled onto their sides and stared behind them, wide-eyed with surprise.

And fear. The sight of a sawed-off shotgun staring down at you can do that.

Al Gray in particular looked like he might piss himself. Melody Thompson did not take the shock exactly in stride, but she did not look as worried as Gray did.

"Stand up, you lovebirds. An' keep your hands where I can see 'em," Longarm said, motioning encouragement with the barrels of his shotgun. "An' you, Al, you can leave your six-gun on the ground there. You won't be needin' it, or at least you won't be havin' it, where you're going. Melody dear, same thing with your rifle. Which I admire, by the way. It's handsome."

Both stood. Reluctantly, but they stood. Both raised their hands, too.

"No need for that," Longarm said. "Put your arms down. You'll tire yourselves t' no purpose if you try and hold 'em